G R JORDAN

Traitor

A Kirsten Stewart Thriller #12

First edition

ISBN: 978-1-915562-54-8

This book was professionally typeset on Reedsy.
Find out more at reedsy.com

We laugh at honour and are shocked to find traitors in our midst.

C. S. Lewis

Contents

Foreword

The events of this book, while based around real locations in the north of Scotland and across the globe, are entirely fictional and all characters do not represent any living or deceased person. All companies are fictitious representations.

Acknowledgement

To Ken, Jean, Colin, Evelyn, John and Rosemary for your work in bringing this novel to completion, your time and effort is deeply appreciated.

Novels by G R Jordan

The Highlands and Islands Detective series (Crime)

Kirsten Stewart Thrillers (Thriller)

Jac Moonshine Thrillers

3. Jac the Pariah

The Contessa Munroe Mysteries (Cozy Mystery)

1. Corpse Reviver
2. Frostbite
3. Cobra's Fang

The Patrick Smythe Series (Crime)

1. The Disappearance of Russell Hadleigh
2. The Graves of Calgary Bay
3. The Fairy Pools Gathering

Austerley & Kirkgordon Series (Fantasy)

1. Crescendo!
2. The Darkness at Dillingham
3. Dagon's Revenge
4. Ship of Doom

Supernatural and Elder Threat Assessment Agency (SETAA) Series (Fantasy)

1. Scarlett O'Meara: Beastmaster

Island Adventures Series (Cosy Fantasy Adventure)

1. Surface Tensions

Dark Wen Series (Horror Fantasy)

1. The Blasphemous Welcome
2. The Demon's Chalice

Chapter 01

The day was frosty, but the sun was shining in the sky. There were no clouds. If you could just get into the direct line of the sun, out of the shade of the trees of the park, you could feel a bit of warmth until the chill of the air fought back against you. Kirsten had never been in Germany, but now, she was standing in a park in Frankfurt, having been taken there by Anna Hunt. They were searching for Gethsemane, someone Godfrey knew—someone Anna had heard of, but only a word, a whisper.

The Service was a mess, undercut by Gethsemane, to where they almost had taken Godfrey. The head of the Service had now disappeared, gone into what Anna had described as ghost mode. She might contact him, but they wouldn't meet him. Everything would be on his terms. He was hiding, something that Kirsten was still coming to terms with. . . Godfrey was afraid.

If Godfrey feared something, Kirsten feared it. Anna certainly feared it, and so did Justin. Justin Chivers had accompanied them and was standing in the other corner of the park as both he and Kirsten watched Anna sit at a public bench. It was made of wood, lovingly crafted, and probably unique.

1

Maybe it remembered someone who had died, or maybe they just had a rather good council here in Frankfurt.

Sommerhoffpark, while not quite taking your breath away, was one of those areas that did a public good—greenery and trees in the middle of a city. There was a friendly atmosphere about it. People were cheerful about being there. Despite the coolness of the air, the sun was bringing in joy. There had been little joy recently in Kirsten's life.

Craig was gone. That's what Anna had said. Kirsten shouldn't treat him now as a long-lost lover, but should treat him as a threat. If she met him, she was never to take her guard down.

Kirsten could see where Anna was coming from. He had certainly changed. Losing his legs had turned him against the Service, turned him against the very thing he'd worked for and believed in for the last ten years. Kirsten wasn't sure if she knew him anymore.

Craig had walked away from her. Well, wheeled away from her. He was still in that wheelchair, and she saw that as something that twisted his mind. He couldn't accept it; couldn't deal with what had happened. She didn't blame him for that, but she blamed him for not trusting in her. She blamed him for not sharing with her, letting his pride impede her from helping him.

And then she felt bad. How do you pour guilt on a paraplegic? How do you blame him for what was going on? He had suffered enough. The fault was at Godfrey's door. After all, it was his mistake to kill an enemy hostage during a prisoner exchange swap that caused all the anger. The anger had manifested itself back towards Craig and Kirsten. That led to Craig being involved in an attempted kidnap and Justin Chivers trying to save him. He had saved him. He just hadn't saved his legs.

Kirsten pushed it all to the back of her mind as she saw an elderly man hobbling along with a stick. She watched as Anna carefully flicked her head over towards him, and then away again, as if she'd seen nothing of interest. Kirsten could tell from the second that Anna had focused on the man that this was he, Klaus Bauer.

Klaus Bauer had been an agent working in Germany for the German equivalent of the British Service. Anna had dealings with him over the years, but he was also the only other person she knew to mention the word Gethsemane. The man was ninety now and Anna had almost felt bad about dragging him along.

Kirsten thought he was doing all right for ninety. Yes, there was silver hair, but he walked reasonably upright, the stick more of a gentle aid than something to hang onto. The man was shuffling along the ground. Certainly, Kirsten could have walked a lot quicker, but he looked all right.

Kirsten let her eyes wander to those people behind Klaus Bauer. She scanned, mentally taking in each person walking here and there. Something in her brain focused on a man at the back.

He was dressed in a blue sweater, beige trousers underneath, and had a rather enormous smile on his face. He was carrying a sports bag over his shoulder and seemed to be nonchalantly walking along through the park. At one point, he got too close to Klaus Bauer. Kirsten looked at him carefully. He was jaunty in his step, too jaunty. Kirsten didn't like it.

She flicked her eyes over towards Justin Chivers and saw that he was staring at someone else. It was a woman jogging through the park, and if Justin had been any other man, Kirsten

3

might have thought he was slacking on the job. This woman was attractive, wearing Lycra. It was extremely luminous. Her hair was tied up in a ponytail with a sweatband; her wrists were covered in sweatbands. She had those rather modern trainers on too, with the short ankle socks, the ones that practically exposed her whole ankle.

But Justin's taste didn't run that way, and Kirsten checked the trajectory the woman was on. Both she and the man would meet Klaus Bauer at roughly the same time. She saw Justin flick his head over towards her, and she gave a quick nod. Together, they walked slowly forward from their positions, moving on an intercept course. She'd take the man around about ten meters behind Klaus Bauer.

The bag was worrying her. Was there a gun in it? It seemed quite heavy for a sports bag. He looked like someone who might have been swimming, or maybe come from a game of squash or badminton, but there were no rackets. The bag was simply too weighed down.

The woman was approaching now at a fair rate, and Kirsten saw the man start to stop and drop the bag down in front of him. Kirsten quickened her pace. She saw Justin doing the same.

Klaus Bauer continued on, unaware of what was behind him, or maybe he knew. Maybe he was aware of the risks. If so, why was he still here? Kirsten couldn't think about that, but she saw Anna Hunt appreciate the danger.

Anna stood up and walked towards Klaus. The man with the bag was now unzipping it, and Kirsten broke into a run. Justin Chivers was further ahead of her. Kirsten saw the handgun being taken out of the bag, about to be thrown up to the woman jogging through.

Chivers was exemplary. He was in a suit with an umbrella, hastening to make the intercept. He arrived at the man just as the woman got there and the man was about to throw a gun up to her. With his left hand, he shoved his umbrella into the man's face and then drove his left shoulder into the woman running forward. He caught her up on the chest. Her pace caught her off guard, and Justin's shoulder was like a wall. She bounced off it straight down and found Justin leaning quickly over her.

The gun had been thrown, though, and it had bounced off the tumbling woman out onto the path. Kirsten clattered into the man with the bag, tumbled forward, picked up the gun, and tucked it inside her jacket. She then went back to the man, apologising profusely, offering to help him up.

'You need to rest,' said Kirsten, and then looked at the man. 'Rest. You need to rest. I'll help you over.'

She picked up the bag, feeling the weight of several weapons inside. Justin still had his umbrella, and he pushed it into the leg of the woman in front of him. Several people were now making their way over.

Kirsten turned to a local, saying to them, 'Do you speak English? I don't speak German. Do you speak English?'

'I speak English,' said a rather helpful man. He was older, with a moustache, and had a concerned face.

'Can you tell this man that I'll help him?'

The man spoke in German. Then the man with a moustache said, 'I can take them to a hospital, if you want. Is he okay?'

'I think he's had a rather large bang on the head,' said Kirsten. 'It might be worthwhile getting it checked out.'

'Is that his bag?' the man asked.

'No,' said Kirsten. 'That's mine. This lady's had a bit of a collision, too.'

'Should I call an ambulance?' asked the man.

'I don't think it's that serious, but concussions need checked out, don't they?' The man looked at her. 'Bangs to the head, I don't know how to say it in German. It comes afterwards.'

The man nodded, and a woman appeared beside him.

'This is my wife. We'll take them to the car and take them to the hospital.'

'Good,' said Kirsten.

The tip of Justin's umbrella was armed with a sedative, and the woman was extremely woozy. Seeing a quick jab from Justin to the man, Kirsten knew he'd be compliant for a while, as would the woman. Justin helped her up and said he would take them to the car.

'My wife can do that.'

'I insist,' said Justin, and Kirsten understood what he was doing. He was making sure there would be no other problems, making sure they were packaged into the car and out of the area. By the time they would come back, no one would be here. Kirsten kept the bag, slinging it over her shoulder. She glanced back towards the seat and saw Anna Hunt in conversation with Klaus Bauer.

Kirsten would remain to stand guard, but the conversation with Bauer wouldn't be long. They were just a couple of people, an old man resting on his way through the park. Justin disappeared, along with the rather helpful man and his wife, ferrying the two victims of the accident back to their car. Life in the park went back to normal, people travelling here and there, young kids playing with balls, families out enjoying a day off, but Kirsten kept a watch.

She'd have to take the bag as well. You couldn't leave

weapons like this sitting around. Maybe she could have given it to Klaus, but at ninety, the bag would weigh him down. The downside of being in Germany was there were no people to drop weapons into, the same as Kirsten did at home. You didn't hang on to every weapon you found. They needed taken out of the public reach.

The conversation with Klaus Bauer took approximately five minutes, and then the old man was up on his feet, walking away without even looking at Kirsten. Anna remained for a moment, then got up and walked away because she had found a coffee cart. She purchased three and then went to a distant part of the park, sitting down on a different bench. Kirsten joined her, slinging the bag underneath the seat and taking a cup off Anna. Justin appeared two minutes later. He'd been about, though, having returned from leaving the attackers in the company of the good Samaritans.

'Did you get anything?' asked Kirsten.

'I got a lot,' said Anna. 'Klaus Bauer is a good man. I told him about the situation we were in. He knows to trust me. That's the thing. As you go on in this life, make sure you leave trust with people. Godfrey hasn't. Godfrey has no one who trusts him now.

'They see me as hard. They see me as someone who can be ruthless, but I'm trustworthy,' said Anna.

'Gethsemane was once believed to be Godfrey's partner by our German friends, but he betrayed her. Klaus says that Godfrey gave her over for a higher prize, although he's not sure what that means. Maybe it's the Service. Maybe he was on his way up. People climb the ladder like that. You need to be aware of that.'

'What happened to her then?' asked Justin.

'The Russians took her,' said Anna. 'Apparently, she suffered a long torture, day after day, horrific. A woman stuck on her own. You can only imagine the way they would torture.'

Kirsten felt the chill run through her. She could imagine, as it nearly happened to her. She was feeling a sympathy for Gethsemane, and then she remembered what was going on back at home.

'But she apparently escaped,' said Anna Hunt. 'She got away. If she got away from that sort of incarceration, she's dangerous. There's few that get away from it.'

'How do you know they didn't just make a deal with her?'

'I don't, but it's very unlikely they just let her get away. They don't make a lot of deals like that. Most people don't turn. Being a double agent's incredibly difficult,' said Anna. 'You've lost everything forever. No one trusts you after that. Even if you come good for them, even if you turn round and offer them everything, they know you jumped ship. You can't jump back.'

'But she escaped then. Is it that difficult?' asked Kirsten.

'It is,' said Anna.

'How do you know?' asked Justin.

'Because I'm one of the few to have done it,' said Anna. 'I didn't like the idea of the torture they were going to put me through. I was lucky. I got out quick.'

Anna went silent for a moment and then she took a large sip of coffee. 'Her last known abode was in St. Petersburg, according to Klaus. He's not sure if she's still working from there, but they know for sure that she was working for a gang lord. Artyom Orlov, nasty piece of work, but not on a government level. That's the trouble with Russia at the moment. Government and gang lords—they all intermix, but she must have been working quietly. Klaus had little information about her. He said it was a rumour, but he said he got it confirmed that she had definitely been there. Where she is now, he doesn't know.'

'Coming to Germany is one thing,' said Justin. 'You really want us to go to Russia?'

'St. Petersburg's not too bad,' said Anna. 'It's got good access via water. You're not in the middle of the country. It's not Moscow.'

'When's the last time you were there?' asked Justin.

'Six years ago,' said Anna, 'but it was a fleeting visit. But if we're decided that we're going to find out about Gethsemane, then this is where we go. . . . So, what's our decision?' said Anna. 'You said you wanted this on an even keel. You're not my employee nor my agent,' she said to Kirsten.

Kirsten turned to Justin. 'And she wants you on the same basis. Do we go?' The pair looked at each other and then Kirsten turned to Anna. 'We go. We go find Gethsemane.'

Chapter 02

St. Petersburg would be a hostile environment, unlike Germany. The trip to Germany had been relatively easy. With Klaus Bauer being contacted, Anna had been pretty sure that the German Service knew they were coming over. Relations between the two organisations had always been cordial, and they'd helped each other in the past. That they were simply turning up for conversation meant that the risk had been absolutely minimal. St. Petersburg would be so very different.

They travelled by boat, deciding to come into St. Petersburg by water rather than land. Anna had picked out a Wildlife Refuge, the Severnoye Poberezh'ye Nevskoy Guby.

No one lived in the wildlife refuge, and it'd be rough going as they wouldn't be using any tents, but wild bags instead to sleep. Anna had contacts in St. Petersburg, and they would be crucial in tracking down an Artyom Orlov. As a gang lord, he would be known, though his movements may be a secret held within his organisation. Russia could be as dangerous a place for the locals as much as any outsider.

They took a small inflatable to the wildlife reserve, pulling it ashore and hiding it in amongst the various grasses and trees. There were no large animals like in a nature reserve back home.

This was a haven for birds, wildlife, and fauna, separated by its island nature from the rest of the Russian mainland. They would need to run over to the coast just outside St. Petersburg before entering the city.

Anna decided that the best thing to do, as she knew the city, was to go alone. One person moving through it would be less obvious than three. Also, if she got caught, she'd have two people on the outside to come and find her.

Kirsten wasn't so sure, but she was operating in foreign territory, and Anna knew the place better than she did. In the dead of night, they pushed her in the boat out to the water and then returned to their sleeping bags, nestled under bushes on the island.

Anna Hunt was dressed in black, but not in her combat fatigues. Instead, she had a jacket that she could spin inside-out with a rather dull green on the inside. She had leggings on that could look classy enough, while also being practical. Inside her jacket, she carried a firearm. Just the one, so as not to raise too much suspicion. She had knives secreted on her, but she was hoping not to make any contact, except for the person she was going to meet.

She took the boat to the north of St. Petersburg, pulling it onto shore and hiding it under a tree. From there, she began the run into town. She came across a house with a small moped sitting outside it. Anna wheeled it away. The owner was hopefully asleep inside the house, for the windows were dark. Once she was clear, Anna started it up and drove into the city.

St. Petersburg had changed little since the last time she was there. She could negotiate the main roads, pass by the rivers, and head out to a rundown area of the city. The blocks were high on either side. She thought about the millions of people who must live here. In a lot of ways, it was a beautiful city with so much history behind it, and yet the building she was coming to was bland.

She parked the moped up outside and walked up to the front door of the block of flats. There was no keypad on it—the door simply opened and she walked up the concrete steps to the fourth floor. She saw several rather bland doorways, each of them green.

Anna clocked the number five. She strode over and tapped on the door gently. No one responded. Anna took out a lock pick from inside her jacket, worked quickly, and had the door open within a minute. She pushed it back and found the flat in darkness.

Anna closed the door gently behind her. Slowly, she glided through the flat. There was a main room with a small old-fashioned television in the corner. The walls had photographs of a woman and several other friends with her, but clearly the woman was the repeating feature. Anna recognised the face.

She swept through to a drab bathroom and found no one inside. Slowly she walked to a bedroom, pushing back the door. From her vantage point in the doorway, she saw two people lying on the bed. She walked over carefully, withdrawing her gun and pointing it at the male figure lying away from her. The female figure was facing Anna, and was breathing easily, deep in sleep. Anna reached down and tapped her on the shoulder. The first time had no effect. The second time the woman woke with a start and Anna slapped her hand over the woman's mouth.

'Easy. Easy. It's me, Laura.'

The woman looked up at Anna, eyes wide open. 'You're

going to get up,' said Anna. 'Put something on. We're going to the next room to talk. Is he okay?'

The woman nodded, and Anna let go of her mouth. The woman rolled out of bed and dressed herself in a gown. Walking through quietly, she put a small light on in the lounge area. She motioned to her seat in the far corner and then stepped across to a bottle of vodka. She poured herself a shot and turned to Anna, who shook her head.

'Business, is it?' the woman whispered. Anna nodded. 'If he wakes up, don't show him any guns. I'll deal with him. Put him back to sleep.'

'Who is he?' asked Anna.

'His name is Max. He's Italian. I do like the foreign types, don't I?'

'Agent?' asked Anna.

'Businessman. But sometimes, you guys use businessmen, don't you? Sometimes they're the way in for the information, but I don't think he is. I think he just likes my body.'

'Fair enough,' said Anna. 'That's not a bad thing.'

The woman tried to look composed, but she was shaking and she downed her vodka in one go before pouring herself another.

'Why are you here?' asked the woman.

'I'm here because I need information. I'm looking for Artyom Orlov.'

The woman froze and shook her head.

'A shake of the head?' said Anna. 'All I get is a shake of the head after what I've done for you?'

'What you did for me was important. He was an abusive man, though.'

'The things he did were not pleasant, and I did it for you, not for my Service. I'm not here on behalf of my people. I'm here for me and I need to see Artyom Orlov. Look, I'm glad you've got someone who isn't treating you the way he did.'

'Let me make a phone call,' said the woman.

Anna nodded. 'In here though,' she said. 'Nowhere else. In here.'

'Do you not trust me?'

'It's been what, six years? No, I don't. I don't trust you. I came here in the dead of night, so I don't trust you.'

'You should trust me, though,' said the woman.

'Do you still work for them?'

'Not too loud,' she said. 'I do some of that work on occasions. They pay well.'

'I hope you haven't found anyone that is too rough.'

The last time Anna had been in St. Petersburg, the woman before her had been someone she'd extracted information from. But when she saw how the woman had been treated by one of the Russian agents she was reporting to, Anna had disposed of him. Everyone said that Anna was truly professional, but if she had been, she would've left the matter. The things the man was doing to the girl were wrong. So wrong that Anna felt, as a woman, she couldn't let it stand. She could do something about it, and she had a few hours to make that happen. No one else had ever known. No one else needed to.

The woman picked up the phone and murmured to the other end. It was in Russian, but Anna understood. 'Where would Artyom be? How would they get hold of him? Were there any significant movements of late?'

It was a network of girls who worked on that side of things. They were useful, because they knew where everybody was going. They knew because people talked to them. Men who shouldn't have said things, and these women shared. They shared it for safety. They shared it to make money because information was always good for money, and they never asked each other what they did with it, because that was safety.

'You know who you're taking on,' said the woman after she'd put the phone down. 'Artyom Orlov's men will shoot on sight. They won't ask questions. They're not the police—they'll just kill you. If they get worried about you, they'll kill you. He won't talk about things either. He's a tough man. I know from my girls that he's a tough man.'

'I've faced a few tough men in my time,' said Anna. 'How do I find him?'

'You don't. He keeps on the move a lot. He's hard to trace, but I know he will be at the theatre. Not tonight, but the night after. His daughter is performing in the ballet. He won't miss it. Dotes on his daughter. He killed her mother, although she probably doesn't know that, and there's no proof of it, but the word is he killed her because she asked for too much. She didn't like what he wanted her to be.'

'Is he like that?'

'She was one of us. He got her pregnant. He liked the baby. She was fortunate in that respect, but then he took a dislike to her because she challenged him. She wanted more, so he dispatched her. He killed her, but away from the daughter. Said she committed suicide, I think.'

Anna made a mental note of it, for it could be useful.

'But he dotes on this girl. She has had only the best and now she's in the ballet; he'll have box seats. He'll go back afterwards to see her and shower her with gifts. It'll be private, away from everyone.'

15

'Which theatre?' asked Anna.

'Alexandrinsky Theatre,' she said. 'It's quite fantastic—small, but beautiful. One thing we do well over here are theatres, the ballet. We can make things look beautiful and yet they build buildings like this,' she said.

There was a sigh from the bedroom next door. Then a voice said, 'Andrea, are you there? Come back.'

Anna watched the woman. She stood up, dropped the gown she was wearing and walked in her bare skin over to the bedroom. She turned to Anna.

'You know I'll help you anytime for what you did for me, but please don't make it a habit. I'm not people like Orlov. If he found out, the things he would do.'

'He won't.'

'Give me a moment,' she said. 'Then when you hear the noises, leave. I'll keep him entertained so he doesn't know you're here. Better that way. Never any questions.'

Anna nodded. The woman opened the door before closing it behind her. Anna sat impassively, thinking on the details she'd heard, and waited until she heard lovemaking in the bedroom. She stood up, exited the room, and then the building, before getting back onto the stolen moped.

At four in the morning, she was making her way back across to the small island where her two partners had spent the night sleeping. They were awake before she found her camp. Anna found her own sleeping bag, wrapped herself up in it as Justin lay beside her.

'Any luck?' asked Kirsten, getting out of the sleeping bag, looking to take a full watch.

'He's at the theatre tomorrow night looking for his daughter in the performance. That's where we'll do it. I've been told they will be private and backstage. We make it work then. It's the only way to do it. Otherwise, everything gets complicated. The fewer complications we have in Russia, the better. We don't have backup, so we need it to run smooth.'

'Run smooth? Do we have the planning for it to run smooth?'

'We know how to improvise.' Anna smiled and then put her head down. She needed some sleep before the planning began.

Chapter 03

The Alexandrinsky Theatre was in the centre of St. Petersburg and the team gathered that afternoon to make their way into the city. They had taken the boat over the previous night and camped out outside the city before slowly making their way in. The plan was for Anna and Kirsten to get backstage. There they would wait within the dressing room of Orlov's daughter, holding her at gunpoint until her father arrived. Then Anna would threaten to kill her unless he spilled the beans about Gethsemane.

Anna felt the plan was a good one, but Kirsten saw a negative side to it. What if he said nothing? What if he called their bluff about killing his daughter? They would not do that. She asked Anna that same question and was relieved when Anna said, of course, they wouldn't.

The other problem was they couldn't kidnap her and take her away and then make further demands. If you weren't prepared to kill the girl on the spot and you then escaped with her, what would that do for you? You'd be running around with a threat they knew you couldn't carry out? Kirsten saw the plan wasn't as foolproof as Anna thought and advised that Justin should remain outside in case they had to work an escape route.

Later that afternoon, they stole a car from outside of town, taking it into the city centre. They parked up some distance away from the theatre. Justin would grab the car that night unless the police were already onto it, in which case he'd have to steal another one.

Getting around within Russia was difficult, and Justin was getting annoyed at how they were constantly operating in fields and bushes. He was used to working in an environment of constant hostility where he was disguised in front of his enemy the whole time. However, Anna said her face was too recognisable. Given what had gone on in the past with Kirsten, she believed she might be as well.

As crowds arrived for the ballet, Kirsten and Anna hung around the rear stage door in a quiet back alley. There were two large men there guarding it. You could get a car into the alley, so it certainly looked like somewhere that people could quietly leave from if they'd been involved in a big performance.

There'd be nobody to bother you. Stars could exit this way. Even Russia had its stars. People weren't that different the world over, thought Kirsten. *We all want somebody to look up to, somebody to dream about, somebody to dream of being.*

Kirsten and Anna waited until the performance was two hours old. Anna had discovered that the running time was approximately two and a half hours, and so the plan was to be in the dressing room after the show had finished. There would be no one around the rear of the theatre. Everyone would be inside enjoying the performance.

Afterwards, they would flood out. Maybe some people would come around to the rear, be prepared to look for an autograph, throw flowers. Then again, Anna wasn't sure that this was that big a performance. Indeed, Orlov was probably only there because of his daughter.

Anna Hunt walked to the rear of the theatre, where the stage door was out of sight. She took off her trousers and her jacket, leaving them on the ground. She pulled her t-shirt up, then it snagged it on her bra at the back. Pulling one side of her underwear down slightly as if it had been harassed, she staggered round to the stage door.

Kirsten waited near the rear of the theatre while Anna protested that she'd been attacked by a man.

'He's still there, attacking my friend,' she said in Russian.

The two bouncers looked at each other before running round to the rear entry. As they stepped round the corner, Kirsten felled them one at a time, driving a punch into each of them. It sent them to the floor, and along with help from Justin, she tied them up.

The pair of bouncers were out cold, and they dragged them along the alley and placed them into the rear yard of a block of flats. Justin covered the men with some tarpaulin that was lying around, and then some rubbish. *They could be out for a while*, thought Kirsten, *but if they come to, the team should be out of here by then*.

Anna redressed and then checked her watch. Kirsten and she stepped inside the stage door, and Kirsten followed Anna as she read the different signs on the various backstage doors. Somebody asked a question and Anna answered it in Russian, Kirsten smiling as they went past. Soon Anna had ushered her into a room.

'This is definitely it?' asked Kirsten.

'This is the star room. It's his daughter's. They know it's his daughter. Even if she's not the star, she's going to be in the best room. That's the way these people work. It's his daughter, and my contact says it's the one he loves, so he'll do that. They are all like this. They spoil them. It's pretty sickening.'

'Pretty weird,' said Kirsten. 'Kills her mother, but loves the girl to bits. People are insane.'

Anna took up a position beside the door. It was ten minutes later that they heard the thunderous applause. Then a young girl opened the door and rushed inside. She was dressed in her ballet tutu, soft shoes, and strappings around her ankles. The girl looked shocked as she saw Kirsten in her room. Before she could scream, Anna Hunt had her hand around the girl's mouth and took her to the far side of the room and put a gun against her head.

She told her in Russian to be quiet, and that if she screamed, Anna would shoot. Anna's gun had a silencer on it so no one would know. Kirsten took up a more forward position, angling across in what was a tight room. There was a knock at the door five minutes later, and then a voice said something in Russian.

'It is her father,' whispered Anna. She hissed something to the girl. The girl blurted out something in Russian. The door opened, and the man rushed in. Kirsten put a gun in his face and closed the door quickly. She stood behind him and he stared at Anna's gun. Anna Hunt held up a finger to her lips.

'Can you speak English?' asked Anna.

'I speak a little,' said the man. 'Why have you got her?'

'We're holding her,' said Anna, 'because we need some information.'

'You'll be dead before you leave the building.'

'I don't think so,' said Anna. 'We're not random kidnappers. We're people who really want to know things, and I want to know about Gethsemane.'

21

The man's face went pale.

'I said, I want to know about Gethsemane,' said Anna in a hushed tone. 'Talk. I know you know her. All the blood's run from your face, so you know her.'

There was a knock at the door and someone else said something in Russian.

'They're asking to come in,' said Anna to Kirsten.

'You,' she said, pointing at the man, 'tell him you want some time with your daughter alone. I speak Russian. Say anything other than that and I'll blow her brains out, followed by yours.'

The man turned to the door, snarled something, and the knocking disappeared.

'You threaten me by holding a gun to my daughter's head. If you ask me about my business, I might tell you. I might make a deal with you. I might say, "How much money are they paying you?" but you're not asking about that. You're asking about someone I can't talk about.'

'Someone you know a lot about,' said Anna. 'I'm holding a gun. I count to five. One.'

The man looked at his daughter, whose eyes were pleading with her father. Kirsten could see tears streaming now, and she was shaking.

'Two,' said Anna calmly.

The man turned away, not looking at his daughter.

'Three,' said Anna. She injected a little more tension into the voice. One of the key things to do at moments like this was to make sure it sounded real. Anna had taught Kirsten this in the past. If you said you were going to kill someone and there was no sign of tension in your voice, it would seem false. You were about to do something that was certainly difficult, after all. People who were calm still felt that extra insecurity about killing someone.

Especially like this, long and drawn out when you're waiting for someone else to say something, when the opportunity is there to take it away. It wasn't like running into a room full of people ready to kill you. You went on instinct in that case. You did it. Bang, bang, bang. Take them down. Don't think. There was plenty of time to think here.

'Four.'

The girl was crying now. If Anna's hand hadn't been over her mouth, she would have pleaded with words to her father, but she pleaded with tears.

'Look at her,' said Kirsten, pushing the gun to the father's head. He stared at her.

'Please, don't,' he said. 'Don't. I can't. If I do, I'm dead. She's dead. The whole family's dead, everyone's . . .'

'Five,' said Anna. The man turned away, covering his eyes with his own hands.

There was a silence. The man turned back and looked at Anna. At first, there were tears as his daughter shook.

'You didn't do it,' he said. 'You're not one of hers. She would have done it. She doesn't hesitate.'

Kirsten pushed the gun again into the back of the man's head, worried that the situation was about to descend.

'We may not kill an innocent girl, but we'll kill you,' said Kirsten. 'Do anything now that threatens our safety and you're dead.' The girl burst into tears again, but the man nodded.

'I am glad,' he said. 'I am glad you're not like her. This one means more to me than . . .'

'Not that much,' said Anna. 'Not that much. You don't know me. You didn't know I wouldn't do that. There was a chance to take a risk with me, taken a risk with Gethsemane.'

'No, I couldn't,' he said. 'I really couldn't.'

Kirsten stared over at Anna, wondering what they did now. It was the one flaw in the plan. If he didn't speak, they would have had to carry out their threat. If they carried out their threat, all they were doing was escaping. They would have had to take him out with them. They could take the girl, threaten to kill her on the way out, but they just showed they wouldn't.

'We're going to go,' said Kirsten, 'and you're coming with us, Orlov.' She turned to the girl. 'You're going to stay here.'

The man spoke something in Russian to his daughter and then turned back to Kirsten. 'She doesn't understand English. I have told her to stay here, not to move, not to say anything until I come back for her. I will come back for her. You can take me with you but let me come back to her.'

'That depends on you,' said Kirsten. 'One step out of line and she doesn't have a father.'

Anna Hunt picked up her phone and sent a message. It would take Justin about three minutes to get the car, and Anna waited.

'If you're going after Gethsemane, understand that you won't find many talking. You won't be able to break people. She instils a fear.'

Well, that's true, thought Kirsten. *Godfrey was afraid, terrified. Godfrey wasn't afraid of a lot.*

'She has her ways and means, but nobody is safe. Your entire family is not safe.'

'Good job we have no families,' said Anna, 'because I distinctly dislike this woman. We will be back. This is not over. We will visit again, and you will give me what I need, but it will be in a place where they don't realise you've given me anything. You will have an option to survive and win at this.'

'You can't do that,' he said. 'Please, you can't.'

'We will survive. Now, if anyone asks on the way out, you tell them to clear our way. If I see a gun, this becomes very bloody,' said Anna, 'and yours will be the first head I blow apart.'

The man nodded. Then Kirsten turned him round to face the door. 'Open it, walk straight back to the stage door entrance. It'll be a left, right downstairs, left again. Keep going to the end. Stop for no one. If anyone's in your way, tell them to get out of it. They'll fear you. They'll just die for me.'

The man turned and said something to his daughter again.

'He's just telling her to stay put, to say nothing,' confirmed Anna.

The man opened the door and then shouted at someone to get out of the way. Kirsten had her gun down low on the man's back, hiding it within her jacket. But maybe some of his people understood because they stepped aside quickly as they made their way out to the stage door exit.

'I won't follow,' he said, 'because I don't want to see you again.'

In the dark of the St. Petersburg night, a car pulled up by the stage door exit and Kirsten allowed Anna to get in first. She then hit the man across the back of the head, causing him to fall, knocked out cold on the ground. She ran down the small steps of the stage door entrance and jumped into the back of the car. Justin Chivers sped off.

'I take it that didn't go that well then?' he asked, routing away from the city.

'You could say that,' said Anna. 'I think we're going to have to become much more creative.'

Chapter 04

Kirsten and the team retreated to the wildlife reserve, lying low for the next few days. They couldn't go back to the UK because they needed to know about Gethsemane. She was the key to all of this. An understanding of their enemy would be crucial to the fight ahead.

Just why was she undermining the Service? If Godfrey had left her behind, just go after Godfrey. It wasn't as if anything would have been sanctioned. It wasn't as if Godfrey had orders to leave her behind.

The days out on the reserve were tough. During daylight hours, they had to stay hidden, keep away from passing boats. The occasional ranger for the islands came to study and record the wildlife. They also were eating thin ration packets brought with them, which could heat automatically. They said they were nutritious, but they didn't taste great.

They were used to working out of premises, but here, there was just nowhere to catch a few moment's rest. At night, one was always on sentry, afraid that someone might see something and pop along to the island. Their boat was well hidden, but even then, if someone came ashore, it left them exposed.

Justin was having to work off a very basic battery, using

his laptop as little as possible, but also making sure he could track communications. Orlov was a gang lord and his communications were easier to get into than the Federal Security Service, or FSB. It still took time, and Justin was worried about what battery he had left. They had brought a few batteries with them and, so far, they had kept the phones and his laptop going, but they would run out soon. Then they'd have to make a move elsewhere.

It was while Kirsten was on sentry duty, standing behind one tree, looking out at a passing boat, that she heard someone crawling up behind her. She crouched down as Justin drew close.

'I've intercepted a general message from Orlov to his men. He said that he's taking the family out on board his yacht towards the Black Sea. I presume that would mean they'll be leaving out of St. Petersburg, from the docks at the harbour front. We could do with getting down there, making sure.'

'Do you know which his yacht is?'

'From some pictures I've seen, it appears to be quite fancy. A super yacht. The guide says it's worth many millions.'

'What are you looking for me to do?' asked Kirsten.

'Best case is to infiltrate the yacht, see what orders have been given. Maybe even find out where exactly he's heading. We could take it out of there, or we could assault the boat on the way out. If we do that, we can keep it going and have time to work on him. His people will believe he's out with his family.'

'Take a wander down to the docks and just have a quick little root around his boat. Is that it?'

'You get all the simple jobs,' said Justin. 'You haven't been trolling through minutiae and emails for the last couple of days.'

27

'Simple jobs?' swore Kirsten under her breath.

'Look at it this way. If he is on the move, we get off this island. I'm sick of eating out of packets.'

Anna appeared behind them. She'd been asleep.

'You move like a herd of wildebeests,' she told Justin. 'What's up?'

Justin relayed the details, and Anna smiled. 'I suggest Kirsten goes on board. She's good at that. I'll take her over, stay close by.'

'Very good,' said Justin. 'I'll get to work, see what else I can find, but my battery's low.'

'Don't sacrifice it and end up losing contact. We may need you,' said Anna. 'Meanwhile, tonight, I and my associate will disappear off to the mainland. Best you get some quick sleep,' she told Kirsten. 'Justin, you can take over in a minute. Keep you off that laptop.'

He grinned at Anna Hunt, but he spent the afternoon on sentry duty.

That night, the small boat disappeared over to the mainland. Travelling in the dark was safer in the sense that they were difficult to spot. However, it left Justin exposed because he couldn't escape without a boat. It was also harder to explain what you were doing running around at night, dressed in black.

Arriving on the other side, Kirsten and Anna walked until they found a car they could steal. It was at the front of the house and they decided to return it on the way back if they got clean away. Driving down to the docks, they stopped some distance away from the main marinas. There were lights along the side of the docks, but also plenty of dark areas to operate from, including some cargo warehouses. Kirsten and Anna routed through them before hunkering down to identify which vessel was Orlov's.

'From the photo Justin had,' said Kirsten, 'I think it's that one. Look at the size of it.'

The boat was like something Kirsten had been on in Argentina. It was the only time in her life she'd seen a private motorboat of such proportions. She'd been on cruise liners, but there were so many people on them. This one was impressive by anyone's standards.

'You can route in via those boats along the jetties; they're not well lit,' said Anna.

'That's what I was thinking. He seems to have a gangway down. Although I'm not seeing any protection.'

'I wouldn't enter that way,' said Anna. 'Somebody like Orlov, he'll have somebody there. He'll have CCTV, something. Try to see if you can climb up the side. I know it's difficult. It looks pretty sheer.'

'Not if you come in from the other yacht,' said Kirsten. 'Where will you be?'

'In the vicinity,' said Anna. 'I'll keep tabs on you as best I can. Signal me if anything happens.'

Kirsten left the cargo shed she was crouched beside and ran over to the start of the marina. She raced across jetties of small boats. Rather than taking the long route round, she jumped from one jetty to the other, eventually arriving at the bigger yacht.

The side of Orlov's boat was indeed sheer, and Kirsten was tempted to run up the gangway through the main entrance onto the boat. Instead, she swung around and climbed up the side of another boat. It was older with many more handholds and when she scrambled up onto the deck, she realised access from the deck was closed off.

This one didn't seem to have much security, if any. In fact, Kirsten believed it to be uninhabited. She stole across the top deck to the side, looking over at Orlov's boat, working out how to get across.

In the backpack she had brought with her was a small grappling hook that could be fired onto other boats. There was a line dropping from it and she would use it to reach the top deck of Orlov's boat, which was definitely uninhabited. There were no lights on inside, but she could see movement down below.

She fired. The grappling hook landed on the top deck and she pulled it tight. Having lined the hook up, and tugging tight the wire across to the boat she was on, she carefully made her way over. Kirsten scrambled along the line until she arrived on the top deck of the other boat.

From there, she unhooked the grapple, lowering it gently off the line as best she could until having to let it drop. It swung and made a casual 'ding' on the side of the other boat. Kirsten waited to see if anybody would react. Someone downstairs came to the edge of the boat and looked around and then, satisfied, went back inside.

The wheelhouse of the Orlov boat was towards the front of it but was also down a couple of decks. Kirsten worked her way down from her position to the deck below, which comprised loungers, a cocktail bar of some sort, and a jacuzzi where the other half lived. She then stepped down some more steps but held her position when a guard walked past.

He was armed, not a handgun, but a machine gun. If he fired that around here, he would blow the place apart. It seemed a crazy weapon for a sentry, especially patrolling somewhere like this. Boats had tight corridors. It'd be awkward to get yourself in a position to fire it, and if you did, you'd have no way of remaining accurate enough to pick off exactly what you wanted.

Kirsten, when he passed, strode behind him, and then moved into another corridor. But then he stopped. He turned and walked back, and she watched him pass from the shadows, before stepping back out into the corridor and following it along towards the bridge.

It was locked. Orlov must have had the boat closed down, just sentries protecting it. If the orders come in, would the course for his trip be plotted yet? Had the captain even been on board?

Taking out some picks, Kirsten broke through easily and then shut the door behind her. She stayed down low as she searched around, occasionally reaching up and taking something off the tables above her. She checked the log books. The last time the boat had been out was three weeks ago.

Kirsten could find nothing, nothing to tell her what was happening. She stood up in one corner, peering around. She heard the sentry coming back down the hallway and let herself sink into the shadows.

Could there be somewhere else? Communications room? Possibly, it might have instructions. Maybe they wouldn't have been brought to the captain yet.

She waited for the sentry to disappear, undid the lock on the door, and stepped out. She followed the corridor back the way she'd come and descended more stairs. There was a plaque up on the side in Russian. She did not know what it said, but there were plenty of ventilation ports for the room. She guessed this might be a communications hub. The door was also locked.

31

Taking her lock picks again, she undid it, stepped in, and saw a myriad of computers and printers. Carefully, she searched through and then found one printer that had paper still in it. She took out the paper, set it down, and photographed it. It appeared to show route destinations. The word 'Pesky' was written. St. Petersburg as well. Anna would have to translate. Clearly, she didn't think her skills were up to much, for she'd sent Kirsten and she couldn't speak a word of Russian. Anna could read this in a glance.

Satisfied she had something, Kirsten replaced the items back in the printer the way they were and took herself out through the door onto the deck, locking it behind her. She followed the path back up, reaching the top deck.

Kirsten now had to get back off the boat. She leaned over the side and saw the sentry patrolling the deck, three levels below. She watched him back and forward, and then he turned tail and went inside. Kirsten made sure her bag was secured around her, stepped off the edge of the boat, and made a large dive for the water below.

The draught of these boats was significant. Kirsten believed she had enough water below her, but it was still a shock when the cold raced past her face. She controlled her descent before swimming upwards. Once she'd broken clear of the water, she slowly swam up to one jetty.

Instead of going back the way she came, she routed another direction, passing several other yachts. She was coming up a set of gangways when she heard someone ahead of her call out in Russian. The man had a life jacket on and a cap of some sort, and a radio attached to that jacket. He shouted again at Kirsten. Then he spoke words which he reckoned would say something like, 'What are you doing here? Identify yourself.'

Kirsten didn't have time for this, but she also couldn't get to him before he would get onto the radio. The last thing they needed was something like this. She didn't want to be picked out as something more than a thief. She put her hands up in the air, and ambled forward.

There was a thud. The man fell down to the ground, and a figure began searching him. She took his wallet, the radio, and a watch off his wrist.

'Come on,' said Anna. 'Time to get out of here. Did you get anything?'

Kirsten nodded. 'It's in the waterproof pack in the bag. Photo of what I think is an itinerary, but you'll need to check it for me. It's in Russian.'

'Why don't you do some work on your languages?'

The pair made their way back to the car they'd taken. Kirsten stripped down as best she could while they drove back to the house and deposited the car. From there, Kirsten dressed again in her cold, still-wet clothes, and they got back to the boat, speeding over to the island before the sun appeared. On arrival, Anna read what Kirsten had found.

'Tomorrow. They head off tomorrow but going up to Pesky; it's up the coast. Seems that they have somewhere up there. That's good,' she told Kirsten. 'We'll be away from St. Petersburg, away from most of his people. There's a chance we might engineer something, but we can't follow them up on this boat. We'll need something bigger, Justin, something that gives us a bit of a cover where we can watch them from a distance.'

'Early start then,' he said. 'I reckon we've got two or three hours before the sun comes up.'

'No early starts,' said Anna. 'Get in the boat. We need to be on the other side before the sun's up'. Kirsten was cold, her wet clothes still on, but she did as instructed. They were back in the boat before Kirsten asked about the next step.

'Plan is?' asked Kirsten.

'People go off to their work. You and I are going to find a house when everybody's out for the day. You could do with a shower, warm up a bit. Justin's going to get us a boat and then we're going on a holiday with the Orlovs.'

'I'm not sure it sounds like a fun holiday to me,' said Kirsten.

'Depends on what boat Justin gets, doesn't it?' said Anna.

Chapter 05

Kirsten and Anna struggled to find a house that was empty but were delighted to see Justin arrive close to shore in a small motorboat. The man had a habit of when working an area of acquiring things. While it was nothing compared to the yacht that the Orlovs travelled in, it was a sensible size. Nothing that would attract too much suspicion. It wasn't particularly fast, but it was normal.

You could imagine a moderately wealthy person trailing up the coast in this, and that was an important look. If anyone approached them, Anna would talk, for her Russian was impeccable, having spent time out here. Kirsten would stay below. Justin, whose Russian was passable if not good, could always assist Anna if necessary.

Kirsten and Anna had been by the shore when they saw Orlov's boat racing up the coast. The man obviously liked the engines to be put on and show the power he had invested in. It was a thing of beauty, but also a monstrosity alongside the smaller boats of the area. There was no way the team would ever catch up with him, but they kept their own vessel motoring along the coast and arrived at Pesky that evening.

The coastline here was rural. There were several houses set

back off the coast. Some of them were particularly large, and the largest one must have belonged to Orlov. This was his territory, his place, after all. Those in the FSB wouldn't have a place like this, but gang lords would.

They kept a watch on the house through the night from the boat. Kirsten was thankful to get a sleep and a wash on board. The following morning, Justin shouted for the women from above deck as he stared along the coastline with binoculars.

'They seem to be coming down to the beach,' he said, 'although there's an entire entourage.'

Kirsten took the binoculars from him, and he was right. Orlov came down to the beach with his daughter, but there were men on either side of him, possibly up to twenty by the time they got down to the beach. The men spread out along the beach, standing and watching as Orlov and his daughter swam out.

Kirsten was surprised at the distance they swam, but they got to a point where they duck-dived. They had masks and snorkels with them, and she wondered what was down below. Anna was already ahead of her and was pulling a chart down from the wheelhouse of the boat.

'It's an old wreck down there,' she said. 'If we're clever, we might instigate something when they're out here.'

'In what way?' asked Justin.

'Well, what we need to do is to get some scuba gear. Mr Chivers, if you can manage that. When they come back, we wait down at the bottom of the wreck until they come out diving, and we keep them down. Make it look like they've drowned, and this time, we threaten the father directly.'

'Okay,' said Justin. 'Good plan. I guess we'll know when Orlov leaves because we won't miss that yacht of his.'

'We certainly won't,' said Anna.

Justin turned the boat around and they headed back into the docks, where they berthed and Justin left to ply his trade. It took him two hours to come back with some scuba gear, putting it onto the boat, and they made their way back up to Pesky. They'd taken the best part of twenty hours to get there and back, and they arrived at lunchtime the next day. They didn't have to wait long, however, before the parade out to the beach happened again.

Maybe his daughter liked the wreck, and Orlov seemed like the doting father. Kirsten and Anna got into the scuba gear and dropped off the rear of the boat. The bow was facing the beach. Out of sight, they swam down. Kirsten swore at the cold of the sea. Yet she was amazed at the number of creatures crawling here and there, the fish swimming past. It took a while until they reached the wreck.

It was reasonably far down, but you could duck-dive it, swim around for a minute or two and get back up. She sat and waited, looking at the barnacled wood around her. She could crawl inside and watch the drifting seaweed and other plant life, some of which had caught on the ruined boat.

It was dark down below, but there was still enough daylight that you could just about see around. A torchlight was shining through the water though, and soon a figure had come down wearing just a mask and flippers, along with a wetsuit. As the figure passed, Kirsten realised it was the girl, and she grabbed her, pulling her close inside the sunken boat.

The girl struggled at first, but then Kirsten shoved a breathing tube into the girl's mouth. The girl was shaken, but she relaxed as she was able to breathe. Kirsten started swapping it over until she saw a figure appear in front of her. Orlov was there.

Seeing Kirsten, he went to swim for the surface, but Anna was above him and held him down. She forced his arms behind him, tied them up, and then slammed the breathing apparatus into his mouth. The pair of them were being held down, and they realised quickly that unless they cooperated, they would not survive.

Once that realisation had happened, it was fairly easy for Kirsten and Anna to swim back with their captives. They rose to their boat, emerging on the far side from the beach. They rolled their captives on board, where Justin covered them with a gun. Anna then steered the boat away.

Nearby was the island of Mayak Seskar. It was a tourist attraction, but it was also the nearest place to get out of the way. Their boat could be moored close by without causing suspicion.

In the depths of the boat, Kirsten had sat Orlov up, tying him to a chair. His daughter had her hands bound and a gag over her mouth, but they were gentle. She wasn't the problem here. Her father would be.

'We're back again,' said Anna to him, 'only this time, we have an advantage. I don't need you to get out of this building. Your girl will be safe. Whatever happens, I'll deposit her on the island while we get out of here. You, however, may not be on the island. You may end up at the bottom of the sea. Distressing for her. Pity for us because you have information that we need.'

Orlov seemed shaken. Maybe it was because they had traced him. Maybe it was because they had come back.

'The thing is, Orlov, nobody needs to know that you've been taken. You swam out here, something went wrong, got disorientated, and you ended up out on the little island, marooned. Now people are going to come, and you'll get rescued. You spent time in the water. A strange current, whatever. You will not disappear on your own. There'll be search parties out soon. These waters will be combed. We'll need to be away from here. We'll either be away from here with two people on that rock or with one person there.'

Anna looked at her watch. 'You're going to tell me in the next ten minutes what you know about Gethsemane. If you tell me, nobody'll ever know it came from you. You never spoke to me. You never had that issue and you'll be safe. I'm going to put a bullet in Gethsemane. You'll be very safe.'

The man looked over at his daughter and then back at Anna.

'You're telling me you will never mention it? You're telling me you think we will be in the clear?'

'They'll hear nothing from us. Hard to put two and two together. We won't even have been here. They don't know who was in the theatre.'

The man nodded. He looked over at his daughter and then turned to Anna and said, 'I'm doing this for her. She needs me. She needs me about. I don't have that much.'

'Tell me what you know.'

'Gethsemane is blonde. She's an older woman in her fifties. Blonde, quite elegant. I got a contact from the FSB. Said I needed to work with her, needed to help her. She was clearing up parts of the city. They asked me to asscss if she was trustworthy. I told them no; she's brutal. She stuck wholly on the tasks she had to do. If I had got in the way, she would have removed me. The FSB, they're the ones who know about her, really. I'm just a gang lord. They say we run this place, but we don't. The FSB runs it. You need to talk to them. They will be the ones who can help you.'

Anna walked up to the man and put her gun under his chin. 'Tell me the rest or I'll blow your head off right now in front of her.'

'No, you won't,' said the man. 'It'll make too much of a mess.'

'The boat's going to be sunk anyway,' said Anna. 'It won't make that much of a mess.'

'His name was Olev Volkoff. He's part of the local FSB. He works in the local headquarters. I take it you can find that. He was the one that put her my way. I don't know what plans they had for her beyond that. I don't know where she came from, but she wasn't Russian. She spoke good Russian. She acted like a Russian, but she wasn't Russian. When I spoke to her, there were things she didn't know, things that a local would say to you.

'She was angry at someone, pissed off, as you say. I didn't ask why she was doing what she did with us. I didn't need to know. Dealings over here, you don't always find everything out. The FSB has been good for me. They let me get away with a lot of things because I have control. Over there, you have your police. You have things like that to control people. We control the people here. We control the money. And we control how things move. That's all I know.'

Anna pushed the gun harder up his chin. The man shook.

'That's all I know. Not in front of her. No, that's all I know.'

Anna thought he was wetting himself. She took the gun away before walking over to Kirsten and whispered quietly in her ear, 'Do you think he's genuine? You think that's it?'

'Makes sense. If they were testing Orlov, they'd test him out with her. Also, be seeing how she works. It's internal. They can soon come down on them both like a ton of bricks. If they lose out and she kills him, big deal. They won't care. Roll up the next gang lord. The story makes sense.'

Kirsten walked over to the girl, untied her hands, and let her run over to her father, who she hugged. Anna didn't remove his bindings. She told the man to stand up. Justin took the boat in close to Mayak Seskar. Kirsten let the pair of them step off. They were both still in their wet suits. She chucked the snorkel masks onto the island as well. He turned, and she cut his bonds, taking the ropes away with her.

'I don't want to see you again,' he said. 'Please don't come near me.'

'We won't. Unless Olev Volkoff doesn't check out,' said Anna. 'The next conversation will be the last one, if that's the case.'

'It won't be,' he said, 'but thank you.'

'For?' asked Anna.

'My daughter's life. Few would.'

'She's an innocent,' said Anna. 'I'm a professional, but I don't kill children. Not unless they're holding a gun.'

The man turned and walked with his daughter up to the centre of the isle, where there was a large red and white fixture with a housed light bulb at the top. He then collapsed on the ground, and she hugged him.

Justin had already turned the vessel away from the island and was making a direct track back to the mainland. If they headed south, they could very well run into all the vessels coming out on the search. So, they went north, further up the coast, even though they'd be coming back to St. Petersburg.

'Looks like the island retreat's over,' said Anna.

'Indeed,' said Kirsten. 'Time to get clever and smart. We'll need to hole up somewhere. We also need to get in and out quickly.'

41

'We're going to need to work out leverage,' said Anna. 'FSB people are different. Gangsters, they shoot each other. FSB man, he's got a career to think of. He doesn't want to be brought down by us, doesn't want to be caught out by his colleagues. Do you know what?' said Anna. 'This next bit is going to be fun.'

'Fun?' muttered Kirsten. 'You have a strange definition of fun.'

Chapter 06

I t took the team two days to set up, as there was plenty to do to cover their tracks. First, Justin sank the boat not far off the coast. The three of them then made their way down into St. Petersburg, initially working out of a derelict building. It was completely abandoned and allowed Anna to work more of her contacts and find a flat within the area. From there, Anna could scout around and discover the building Olev Volkoff worked in. The FSB didn't advertise to the general public where they were, but, as at home, people within the various organisations knew, so word always got out. Secret buildings weren't that secret to those in the know.

The difficulty was that Anna needed to know where Olev Volkoff would really be. It was one thing to say he worked from that building. But did he, or was that just a story held up? When he really wanted to work, did he disappear elsewhere? Anna worked out of many places, so she would need to find out.

With her ability to speak Russian, it made sense that Anna should be out on the streets trying to find an FSB mark whom she could intimidate. She knew certain streets where they sought their prostitutes. However, these were slightly fancier women who would disappear back to a hotel and would keep their lips sealed if ever questioned. A lot of the FSB had wives at home, and they didn't want their dirty laundry dragged back there.

Anna took up residence around those streets for a couple of nights. Rather than trying to pick someone up, she would watch them, stalking around to see who was coming, trying to pick out a mark. She needed someone who had little money. Someone who was happy to take instruction about where to go, not demand that they went back to a specific hotel. She'd always wondered what it was about people with power. Why did they seem to have a sexual appetite as well? It was true. It was true for her too, even though she had learned to tame it.

It was one thing to be the way you were. However, it was another thing to let it control you. Going out and picking up women in this fashion was allowing yourself to be controlled. You were doing something you didn't want to get caught with at home. It was probably worse than anything you got caught with at work. Work would overlook this, unless you'd been out with an agent from the other side. That was unforgivable.

It was on the second night that Anna spotted her mark. The man seemed to wonder about whom to choose. He got turned down by a few of the women as well, and Anna wasn't sure why. He'd been there both nights and so far, he'd not disappeared with anyone.

Anna retreated to the flat the team had been in and went shopping the next day. She had a blouse that made sure that her ample charms were on view. She had a skirt that was so short, she'd be embarrassed by it back home. Stiletto heels. She had a jacket where no significant view was covered up. She'd picked wisely, for it also concealed her gun. That night, she turned down offers from three men before she spotted her mark. He pulled up close in the vehicle, letting the window wind down.

'Like what you see?' she said in Russian.

'Very much,' he said. 'Do you like being entertained?'

Anna thought she wasn't picking up the translation for a moment, so she asked, 'What sort of entertainment?'

'I like to get kinky,' he said. He motioned to the seat beside him where there was a suitcase.

'What's in there?' asked Anna. He opened it up to reveal ropes and chains. 'I like a woman to behave herself,' he said. 'I like to punish her when she doesn't.'

'Put the suitcase in the boot,' she said, 'and I'll come, but to a hotel room, not back at your flat,' she said. 'I'm not here to be killed.'

'No', he said. 'You're just here for a little instruction.'

Anna felt her flesh crawl at the thought of it. He got out, put the suitcase away, and she joined him in the front of the vehicle. He kept staring at her as he drove to a hotel. She knew Kirsten would be somewhere watching. At that time of night Kirsten could move around the street unseen and it gave her a bit of comfort. Anna was worried about this individual.

He took her through to a hotel where there was a nod from the concierge, a cheeky smile between the two men. A rather drab lift took them up to an even more drab corridor, where the occasional bit of wallpaper was peeling off. She thought she'd entered a 70s room when she saw it. The man had the suitcase with him and he opened it up on the bed.

'How much?' he asked.

It nearly caught Anna out. She hadn't even thought about it. 'How much do you think I'm worth?' she asked. He told her in Russian and she gave the idea that she was thinking about it for a moment and then she nodded her agreement. She took off her jacket and then her blouse before removing the skirt to stand in stockings and her bra.

'Are you going to remove those as well?' he said.

'I thought I'd let you do that, but maybe you want to discipline me first.'

She put her hands out in front, but he instead moved them behind her. Anna felt the handcuffs go on. She'd seen the type. Recognised them for what they were. If you knew what you were doing, you could release them. There was a quick catch. They were play handcuffs after all. Maybe the man didn't realise that or maybe he did, just hoped that the women wouldn't. He reached inside the suitcase, telling Anna to get on her knees. She saw him withdraw a whip.

'What do you intend to do with that?'

'Whip you till you bleed', he said. The next word was colloquial, but she thought the word 'slut' would've been close. He moved his arm back, ready to crack the whip.

The handcuffs dropped off her wrists. She rolled forward, surprising him, and drove up from the floor with a hand grabbing him by the throat. Her other hand twisted his wrist, forcing the whip to drop, and she planted him into a chair in the corner. Her hand went over his mouth and she sat on his knees, stopping him from kicking his feet. She choked him so hard he rasped, trying to talk.

Anna hit him with a punch to the face, causing his nose to go bloody. She quickly turned, walked to her jacket, took out her gun, and pointed it at him.

'I believe you're a member of the FSB,' she said. 'You have that way about you, and I've been watching you for several days. Your people won't be thrilled about that. Maybe they need to know. Maybe they don't. I won't just shoot you. I'll make sure you get handed over with every tale about how you failed to spot me. What you've told me. It will all be lies, of course, but they won't know that. They'll rip you apart. Either that or they'll beat you. They'll force out of you what you did actually tell me, but you'll be practically dead before they realise you told me nothing. I've done this before. I am no amateur. Your best bet is to play ball with me, to tell me what I want to know.'

Anna could see the man was scared. He was shaking, and she was waiting for him to wet himself or to do something similar.

'Understand, if you shout out, I'll put a bullet through your head, a second one, and then I'll throw your body out that window. I'll be long gone before anybody comes to rescue you. I don't think the FSB are watching this one, are they? They won't be. I don't think they like people like you with these other pleasures. It makes you too easy to get hold of. You hide that away, don't you? Oh, they don't mind someone that likes a bit on the side, but you take the classier girls. The ones that don't talk. The ones that are from here. I know how the game is played.'

'What do you need to know?' he asked. Anna stepped forward, took the whip off the floor, and cracked it. The man jumped.

'Of course, they need to hear the whip going because they'll be used to it here, to the odd bit of pain.' Anna let go a sudden shout. 'Used to hearing the women shout like that, don't they? I could shoot you right now for what you are, and I wouldn't bat an eyelid. It wouldn't bother me in the slightest, really.

47

That's not what I want. Olev Volkoff. Tell me about Olev Volkoff.'

The man's face suddenly went white.

'Yes, Olev Volkoff,' said Anna. 'It's up to you. You can tell me and you can go back to your career. You can even come back to doing this nonsense. Or you don't tell me, and your career will be over and I'll beat you to a pulp. Then I'll get somebody else to tell me about Olev Volkoff. You could turn around and tell them, "but I was intercepted by this agent." For that, they'll throw you out as well. You're in a no-win situation. The only way you walk out of here with your life is if you talk to me properly. Otherwise, your life is about to end in one of two ways: with a bullet, or an FSB cell at the back end of nowhere, tortured for the rest of your life to find out what you said.'

Anna wasn't sure that all of that was completely true, but the man's face showed he believed it.

'I know little about Volkoff.'

'You better learn quickly,' said Anna.

'He's too high up.'

'What do you know, though? Where does he work?'

'At HQ, in town. He has a desk there near the top.'

'No', said Anna. 'I want to know where he works. That's just where he goes in for formal meetings. Where does he actually work? Where do you get hold of him if you need to, and it's not a formal day?'

The man's shoulders shrunk in somewhat. She could read the fear all over his face.

'He has somewhere. It's a simple place.'

'How do you know?' asked Anna. 'You could lead me down the path.'

'No, I courier packages to him where they need to be. I

despatch documents. That's my role. It's not a prominent role, but I have to be security-cleared for it. I have to know where people are. But it's only on the day I get told where they are. I don't know beyond that. Several times I have gone to the Avtovskyia Ulitsa. I think he has a flat there. When I delivered things to him, I was brought inside once. There was a desk and an office that clearly had somewhere else for an assistant to be. In the back of the building, I saw there was a bedroom. There was a kitchen, too. It wasn't a set of offices. It was a place to stay.'

That was interesting, thought Anna.

'When was the last time you delivered to him?' she asked.

'Three weeks ago,' he said. 'He isn't usually in the headquarters. He's in maybe once, twice a week when there are the big meetings. Outside of that, he's not there. I think he must work from Avtovskyia Ulitsa because I don't deliver packages to him anywhere else.'

'How often do you deliver them to him?'

'Once a month,' said the man. Anna cracked a whip again. The man nearly jumped.

'Have you ever been hit with one of these?' she said.

'No,' said the man.

'What does it do?'

'What do you mean, what does it do?' he said.

'Tell me what it does!'

'It can break the flesh. It leaves a mark, at least. The ones I have, they break the flesh.'

'You take women up here and hit them with this? Then what? Have sex with them?'

'I rarely have sex,' he said. 'Yes, I hit them. It rarely takes sex.'

Anna raised her gun to the man's head. For every woman

alive, she wanted to put a bullet in the man's head to end him. Instead, she stepped back and told him to stand up. He did so, and she told him to undo his shirt. He did the same. After telling him to remove it, she stared at his bare back. The whip cracked again. A line of blood grew across his back. She cracked it five more times.

'Put your shirt back on,' she said. Suddenly tears were coming from her eyes and the man stared at her. Her makeup was running, and she hobbled.

'I guess the women who leave from here look like this, don't they? Because that's what we're doing. We're walking out of here. Any funny stuff and I will kill you and disappear into the night. You tell anybody at the FSB.' She stopped. 'Oh, yes,' she said, 'if you tell anybody at the FSB, you're as good as dead, anyway. They'll torture you for what you probably said to me, and when they find out what you did, they'll dispose of you.'

The pair left the hotel, Anna still in tears as she walked past the concierge. He smiled at the man. They got into his car outside and he drove her back to the street. Anna had stopped her crying.

'I'll be watching,' she said, as she stepped out of the car. 'You won't see me coming.'

The man drove off, and Anna hobbled around several streets until Kirsten found her.

'Are you okay?' she said.

'Fine,' she said. 'Crocodile tears. Had to do it for the act.'

'Any joy?'

'Oh, yes,' she said. 'Avtovskyia Ulitsa, that's where we're going, and we need to move. In fact, I feel like we should go for it tonight.'

Chapter 07

I t had just gone midnight when the team arrived in the Avtovskyia Ulitsa area. The area was rather mundane. Some housing, a few shops, and everything rather drab. Kirsten was finding Russia to be strange. There were great stretches of beauty. There were some fantastic buildings within cities, but on the outskirts, parts of it were so mundane.

Maybe this was just St. Petersburg, for Russia was such a large place, and St. Petersburg, a city of tradition. She struggled sometimes, seeing the finery alongside the common. Then again, wasn't every city like that? Was the world really that different wherever you went? Kirsten wasn't so sure.

The street light was dim as the three drove past the building of Olev Volkov. They drove past it only the once, parking up several streets away. There was a large tree that seemed to block out one of the main streetlamps. The car was shrouded in darkness.

'I'll get closer,' said Anna. 'If I'm not back in five, come get me.'

Anna stepped out, now with a leather jacket zipped up tight around her, and also in black leggings. She wore a balaclava on her head, except it was rolled up, so it looked like a beanie hat, ready to be dropped at any moment. She walked closer. Realising that the streetlight at the front of the building meant being displayed on any CCTV cameras, she dropped the balaclava. She also jumped into the rear gardens of the buildings.

It took Anna only a couple of minutes to be within sight of the building in question, and she could see a light on in the bedroom. The curtains were only partially closed, and then she saw a man looking out. He stared around the grounds, this way and that, before turning back, a pair of arms suddenly coming around the back of his shoulders. *It was him*, she thought. *If it's not him, somebody's using his bedroom. Somebody's using his apartment. That could work as well.*

Anna raced back to the car, telling the rest of the team that it was on. Justin told the women to remain, and he checked out the security arrangements around the building. It would be another one of those situations where you didn't want too many security cameras. If you put too much up, everybody would know someone of importance operated from there. One problem faced by the Service, wherever it went. Any Service.

Justin returned ten minutes later, advising there were alarms on the windows and on the doors set to trigger recordings inside. However, he saw nothing disappearing out to an external source, although it could be remotely tripped. They'd have to move fast.

Kirsten and Anna stole into the rear garden of the building. They had to climb through three others, utilising trees to drop in and wait in the darkness. There was a rear door, small, with some rubbish collected close to it. Maybe all the flats didn't belong to Olev, then. Or maybe they did. Maybe this is how they based things. You could do that. Own all the flats, so you would base staff in different ones. The offices would be here and there amongst them, but from the outside, they would just look like normal accommodations. Kirsten had seen a few of those back in the UK.

The rain fell. Justin appeared in view, leaning over the fence of a nearby garden. He gave the thumbs up. Everything would be disabled. Slowly, the two women stepped across and opened the rear door.

Inside was dark—not a single light—and they crept slowly forward. The stairs up the middle of the building were concrete with an untidy finish, a metal banister on either side. Kirsten crouched at the bottom, trying to stare up at the gap at the side to see if anyone was looking down.

He didn't really run like this, did he? she thought. *He must have guards of some sort. After all, he was a reasonably high-up figure.*

She gave Anna the thumbs up, and Anna stole quickly up the first set of steps before looking up for the next. She signalled back to Kirsten. There was someone there. Kirsten crept up beside Anna, looked up, and saw the shadows in the darkness. It was a man, dressed in shirt and trousers. He was smoking a cigarette and walking back and forward. The two women looked at each other.

The plan was to get to Olev. Maybe they needed to bring him away with them. It would be difficult to work from a distance, coming back and forward to him. Capture and release within the next day would be the best option.

Carefully, Kirsten crept up the stairs. While the man watched out of the windows, she got up close behind him and hit a nerve in his neck. He dropped towards the ground, and she caught him, laying him down gently. Anna stole past her, looking up the next set of steps, and the ones after that, waving Kirsten up.

They reached the floor that the light had been on, and Anna carefully approached what Kirsten believed was Olev's flat. There was Russian writing, and Anna turned round and gave a nod to Kirsten, showing this was it. They tested the door, but it was locked. Anna stood guard while Kirsten worked with her picks at the lock. It took her a moment before she was opening the door and they swept into the flat of Olev Volkov.

There were photographs everywhere. Photographs of family in the main. Probably, these were his wife and his children. The small corridor led to a room on the left, which Kirsten had opened to see a small desk and many filing cabinets around it. It too had photographs, but not of the same family. Just a single woman with a boy. The woman was older, maybe in her forties. Kirsten noted that she'd certainly kept her looks. She was tall and shapely, and clearly very proud of her son. Her blonde hair fanned out across her shoulders in several photos.

The pair stepped away, back into the main hallway, and opened another door to find a comfortable seating area. It had magazines on one side. It gave Kirsten the feel of a doctor's waiting room. Again, there was the odd photo here, but this time it was back to the family. The man in the photos they recognised as Olev Volkov. Justin had provided pictures previously.

It must have been a secretary's room, previously, she thought. She was on that side of the corridor. *Everybody waits in here.*

Kirsten stepped forward through the door at the end of the hallway and found a large spacious office. There was a desk that must have taken several people to bring into the building, much bigger than the drabness the building deserved. There was a picture of family again, but also some Russian generals.

Kirsten noted the room had only one window, which had blinds pulled across it. Off to the left was another door that lay ajar, and she thought she could see a kitchen through there. Then, two other doors, one of which had light emanating from underneath it. Kirsten crept over, bent down by the door, and listened.

Physical exertion was taking place, and Kirsten pointed to the door, showing Anna that Volkov was in there. They quickly checked the other bedroom. It was plain; somewhere to stay over. A single bed. They routed through into the kitchenette, found a couple of bottles of wine and the dishes from a meal unwashed. When they sniffed the air, there were traces of thyme and basil.

Kirsten whispered in Anna's ear, 'Do you think he's got his mistress in there?'

She nodded. Together, the two of them approached the door to the bedroom. The plan would be to go in quick, and if they were in the throes of anything, it would be easy to hold them at gunpoint. There'd be no quick reaction back. Always careful to play the game in case it was being used against them, Anna and Kirsten would burst in with guns up, ready to take down anyone pointing one back at them.

Kirsten turned the handle of the door, swinging it open, but it didn't make a creak. The two women stepped in to find the lovers were facing away from them. At first, they were oblivious, carrying on with their lovemaking.

Kirsten and Anna entered the room. Anna took her phone and started filming what was going on. She ambled round to the side, capturing the faces of those too distracted by their own efforts to notice her. When she came round into their eyeline, there were shocked faces.

The man was indeed Olev Volkov, and he jumped back, hand going to his face, his other hand disappearing down to his nether regions, not knowing quite what to do. He spun, turning, presumably to grab a weapon from somewhere, but Kirsten held a gun in his face. His hands moved up slowly.

The woman turned and looked up at Anna. It was the secretary from the pictures. The two lovers stood, captured in their moment, with hands up. Anna spoke to them in Russian, telling the woman to put something on and showing that the man should dress. He was definitely coming with them, but she was unsure what to do with the secretary. They left the light on in the bedroom and took Olev and the secretary through to the waiting room at the front of the apartment. There they sat them down, arms untied and free, but guns trained on them.

'You can't,' said Olev in Russian. Kirsten watched as Anna took over the conversation.

'We can.'

'It's my wife, isn't it? My wife has sent you. An all-woman team to come and get me. She's known for a while. She's known. Her father will kill me. He's the genuine power. The money. He has influence.'

'But that's who's paying us,' said Anna. 'We're being paid to bring this evidence to her. We can just walk now, but I thought it best for us to have a chat just in case you want to offer us something extra.'

'Whatever you need,' said the man.

'Money,' said Anna, 'we deal with money. We're doing this for the money. If you can offer more money, I will, of course, see things in a different light. This is some striking video, though. You're rather nimble for your age.'

The man sat, wondering if he should be flattered by what Anna said, but his gut was sitting over the top of his belt. He certainly didn't have a figure that would suggest any physical strength. Clearly, he didn't work out, except with a wine bottle, and Anna wondered what the woman saw in him. She looked like a woman in trim. Someone who looked after herself.

Was it the power? Was it the opportunity? There was quite a risk going to bed with someone like this. Would he just ditch her?

'But you can't tell her. I'd have to get Victoria out of here. She has her son to think of. My wife would . . . my wife would kill them both. She's bitter that way.'

You are the one doing the dirty behind her back, thought Anna, *but not to worry.* 'We can help you,' said Anna, 'for the right sum of money.'

'It'll take me time to get it together,' said the man.

'Then, in that case, come with us.'

'No,' he said desperately, putting his hands up.

'Just as an insurance policy,' said Anna. 'You come with us quietly, and we go somewhere where you can make your phone calls; you can organise the money. We'll take it. You come back. You're part of the FSB. Of course, you might have to disappear. We'll let Victoria go back to her son, but someone will watch, and she can come in here and act as normal.'

The man was desperate, clearly.

'Okay,' he said. 'Okay, but we need to cover up. We need to . . .'

'You need to sit here,' said Anna. 'I will leave my colleague who doesn't speak Russian, and she will shoot if you move. I'll go through with Victoria, who will clean up and put everything back the way it should be, and she will turn up for work in the morning. We'll leave the building quietly.'

It took about half an hour for Victoria to do all the dishes, switch off the light in the bedroom, placing the covers back. She dressed and looked like she had stayed on after office hours, for her outfit suggested only that of a secretarial propriety.

It took five minutes to walk out of the building, flag down Justin, who looked amazed, and then take Victoria to her home, where she was dropped off. The team then drove, with Olev Volkov in the car, back to their secure base. It had gone well and Anna was happy, but the truth would come out now. Could they break the man? Could they get their information on Gethsemane?

Chapter 08

Justin Chivers heated some water on a gas cooker. The inside of the building was rough, but the facilities worked. There were a couple of cracked mugs, and he was able to make some percolated coffee. The three agents sat down opposite Olev. He was hanging his head in his hands.

'How much do you want?' he asked suddenly, in Russian.

'He's asking how much we want,' said Anna to the others. Anna stood up, strode over to Olev, knelt down in front of him and lifted his chin up. 'It's much worse than that,' she said to him. 'We're not here for the money. We're here to find out about a woman. Her name is Gethsemane'

His face went white. 'No,' he said, 'no. You can't ask me about her.'

'She's what we want to know. If you don't tell us about her, your wife will see the video. I have no qualms,' said Anna. 'I am not from here. Just an agent with a problem with Gethsemane. I need to know about her now. You have got the time it takes me to drink my coffee to tell me. Otherwise, the film will be sent to the FSB, and more importantly, to your wife. We'll show your office is being breached. We'll tell them you squealed like a pig. There'll be no coming back,' she said. 'However, if you

59

tell us about Gethsemane, we'll leave. I have no need or desire to destroy you, but if that's the only way I get my information, then that's what I'll do.'

The man stood up, walking back and forward. He swept his hand through his hair, a cold sweat appearing across his face.

'If I tell you, it can't come out. If I tell you, it needs to be like I never saw you. She would finish me. She would finish anyone. Victoria would be at risk.'

'We don't want to risk Victoria and her son, do we?' said Anna. 'It's up to you. Think hard on it. I'm going to drink my coffee.'

Anna turned and saw Justin smile at her. He got the gist of the conversation. Kirsten was looking bemused. Anna leaned in close and whispered in her ear.

'He fears Gethsemane. He's working out whether he can trust us to keep it quiet. However, he's not sure he can.'

Anna Hunt sat opposite, slowly sipping her coffee, staring at Olev. Every time he lifted his head, she was looking at him before peering into her coffee cup. Then she put it down, stood up, and put on her leather jacket.

'Where are you going?' he asked.

'I'm going to do what I said I would do,' Anna retorted. 'Won't take long.'

'Don't!' he said. 'Don't! I'll talk to you, but you have to keep it quiet. I need to walk away from this. You see that.'

'You need to trust me then,' said Anna. 'I am a very trustworthy person. I demand a lot from people, but I'm trustworthy. Aren't I?' She turned and looked at Kirsten, who had no idea what Anna had been saying because the conversation was in Russian. Kirsten nodded anyway. Anna turned back and smiled at Olev. 'So, what do you know?'

'She's not a pleasant woman. She's very attractive. Even now she's in her fifties.'

'Ideal for you,' Anna said. 'Victoria is heading towards fifty.'

'I do like them tall. Victoria, though, it's more than looks. She's loyal. You don't get that in my job. Loyalty isn't anything.'

'Tell me more about Gethsemane,' said Anna.

'I don't know her real name. I am too low for that. But I had to help her and work with her here. Often, she goes around with black hair, but she's a redhead. She's about fifty. Everywhere she goes, there are protectors. She had a trio of them here, much younger, like boys. The queen bee with her workers around her. She speaks with a Russian accent. She talks as if she's been here for years.'

'Been here?' said Anna. 'You don't think she is Russian?'

'She's not Russian. Definitely not Russian. We have ways of working in Russia. We are sad people at times. Worn down by hardship. We do what's necessary, but a lot of us, we don't delight in it. It just comes down to you and them. You don't do it, somebody will do it to you. Rather grim, I know. Whereas you have a glamour about you. You're from the West. I can see that now. Now you're speaking more to me, I understand. Your Russian is good, very good, but like Gethsemane, it's not from here.'

'What was your role with her?' asked Anna.

'She was helping me root out American spies in St. Petersburg. We had an influx, and the higher echelons sent her along to assist. She was very good at it. Very good. We rounded up a lot. She could extract information, but her methods were . . .'

He stood and wiped his sweat off his palms against his backside. 'If she catches me, if you see her go for me and you're about, just kill me. Better that than what she does to people.'

'You would think she would be a bit more restrained than that. Coming from the higher-up echelons.'

'She's not FSB. Gethsemane doesn't have the mannerisms of someone in the FSB. No, she's separate. She's brought in, she's a . . .'

'A pawn, like in chess?' offered Anna.

'Not the pawn. More like a knight or a bishop. Someone you'd be sad to lose, but someone who can damage.'

'Do you think she was paid?' asked Anna.

'She was paid. Handsomely too. Handsomely paid to hurt some poor bastard. I had to sit in on some interrogations. What she did to the men and to the women . . . one man, I remember. Jeffrey. Jeffrey, she said his name was. He was only in his twenties. I'm not sure if he'd been tortured before. I put him out of his misery in the end. There was nothing left of him.'

'Godfrey,' said Kirsten suddenly. 'What's he saying about Godfrey?'

Olev looked over at her. Then back at Anna. 'He's not saying Godfrey, he's saying Jeffrey,' said Anna in English. 'But with the accent, it sounds like Godfrey, doesn't it? He's saying that she really hurt someone. He was called Jeffrey.'

'The earlier story ties in—the one about Godfrey leaving her. Sounds like she's not over then,' said Kirsten.

'Do you think?' said Justin. 'See what else he knows.'

'What do you know outside of the operation she was involved in?' asked Anna. 'I need more. I need to know more about her.'

'Look, I don't know that much more about her. I could tell you about the agents we were involved with, the ones we rounded up. I could tell you how she came up with names and places from her own team. Things I never heard. I could tell you how we buried the bodies and took heat from the Americans for months afterwards.'

'Where is she now?'

'I don't know. They brought her back. They took her back inside the higher echelons. She was loaned out to me,' said Olev, 'except it's one of those loans that you're forced to take. It was suggested that she would help. Suggesting it was a command. I didn't enjoy having her about. People like that— they're not people. You're a person. Well, you're not a good person. You're doing this. Like me, you're not good. But we have a code. You've put Victoria back. She has a son. You didn't kill her unnecessarily.

'Jeffrey had a son. There was not much to be extracted from him. He was young. Bottom of the food chain. He gave up what he knew in the space of ten minutes. The rest of it. The rest of it she did to hurt him. Why? Why did she do that? Is she a sadist? Is she just someone who doesn't like young men, or just men?'

Olev was stalking about the room now, and Anna stood up, telling him to calm down. 'Take a seat,' she said. 'Take a seat. We're not done. I need to know more. I need to know more or I'm going to have to release that video.'

'I don't know more,' he said. 'Just worked with her here. I can tell you all the details about here, what she did in St. Petersburg.'

'I don't want to know about St. Petersburg. I want to know about her. Want to know where she's come from. I want to know who she works with. Where she is now. I need to know everything about her. Not the past, the present.'

'Please,' said Olev. 'Please. I need to—I need that video. I am a dead man without it.'

'Then you need to tell me how we're going to get to know more about Gethsemane,' said Anna. 'I'm a reasonable woman. Get me what I want, and I'll send you back and you can plan to run off with Victoria. You can get out of the country. You'll have ways to do that, I know. Or you can live your sham. It's up to you. I don't care. What I care about is Gethsemane.'

The man stood up again. He walked over towards Justin, indicating he would like a cigarette, but Justin didn't smoke. He turned back and started rifling through his coat. Kirsten withdrew a weapon, pointing it at him.

'I don't have any weapons. You've searched me,' he said in Russian.

Anna waved Kirsten down. A single cigarette was pulled out of the depths of the jacket pocket. He lit it, walking over to the window and calmly smoking. In the dim light of the room, a trail of smoke rose to the ceiling. There was a tension, though, a tension that could be felt by everyone. The trio had risked so much in trying to obtain this information. If he couldn't get any more, where do they go? The trail was dead. She'd been here, though, and they'd have to dig up more, but from where? It would be hard piecing everything together and time was against them back home. They'd been away already for quite some time. Olev turned.

'I won't lie to you,' he said. 'I really won't lie to you. It'll be risky. You want to know why. I need to work out a cover story.'

'Who?' asked Anna, realising there was another source of information.

'Morozov, Ivan Morozov. My superior. He was party to

much more information. He gets to see things naturally.'

'Would you be able to set up a meeting?' asked Anna.

'I could, but how? What do we do? What reason do I have for saying, "Talk to these people?" That's the problem. I can give you the person who would know, but . . .'

'A meeting?' said Anna. 'We could do with a meeting. Maybe I have information?' said Anna.

'I need to show the trail,' said Olev. 'I need to show where it's come from. If you were working back home and you brought someone saying, "I have information from a source you don't know," you would get asked questions. You know this. I need to think about it. I need to make up a decent story, but if anyone in St. Petersburg will know, it will be Morozov.

'I hate him. You know that? I hate him. He's arrogant. He calls me the little man. Every time I'm in the room, it's the little man.'

'We need to meet,' said Anna. 'We need to meet. You organise a meeting, and I promise you, I will not let that video out. Victoria and her son will be safe. You will still live with a woman who wants to kill you if she finds out your infidelity, but that is your business,' said Anna. 'Get me a meeting. Can you do it?'

The man drew in from the cigarette and blew out some smoke. He turned and walked away for a moment, taking the drags from the cigarette like it was the last one he would ever smoke. He turned back, threw it onto the wooden floor, and stamped it out.

'I can do it,' he said. 'I can't guarantee that Morozov will go for it. He may not believe me, but I'll do it if you don't show that video.'

'You have a deal,' said Anna. 'Put it into play.'

65

She turned and looked at her two colleagues. It wasn't ideal, far from perfect, but she'd get to meet Morozov. If necessary, she'd bring him here and get the truth out of him.

Chapter 09

Kirsten sat in the small boat as it putted along the river, heading for the Volodarsky Bridge in Saint Petersburg. Olev Volkof had come through on his promise and had set up a meeting with Ivan Morozov on top of the bridge. He said that Anna, using the code name Maria, had information about American spies within Saint Petersburg. They had been identified, he had told Morozov.

It definitely piqued Morozov's interest and Olev was able to arrange a meeting for midnight on top of the bridge. It was an open space, somewhere it would be difficult to escape from, but it was a risk that Anna was prepared to take. She knew Olev was taking a risk himself, for there was no information. Maybe the man would already have been done away with.

The night air was frosty, especially as the boat putted along the river. Justin would remain in the boat while Kirsten and Anna took to the bridge to meet Morozov. He was expecting them to approach from the road, but they'd come up via the stanchions, hopefully wrong-footing the man. If they were good, they might capture him because Anna was not of the belief that he would volunteer information about Gethsemane to people he didn't know.

There was also a better chance of performing a snatch and grab than trying to pick him up from his own abode or his offices, for they would be guarded. He wasn't Olev. He was higher up. The higher up you got, the more you looked after yourself. Godfrey, prior to this insurrection, always had people about.

The head of the Service had people like Brenda, even though Brenda had turned on him. Even now, Godfrey could go into hiding. The higher up the chain, the better their backup plans. They weren't like Olev, getting caught in bed with his mistress, his secretary. The man was an amateur. Anna did not hold out the same hope for Morozov.

The river was wide as Justin stopped short of the bridge beside a bank. The women would swim over and the wind that was howling would cover their approach. They were in black tight clothing, and without a gun, but Anna and Kirsten had enough weapons on them. Knives to throw and also a couple of flash-bangs.

The gear they'd brought from the UK was nearly done and Anna was getting edgy, for it was time to get back home. Tonight needed to go well.

Kirsten dropped into the water quietly, Anna then followed. They felt the cold seep through the clothing. Kirsten didn't think it was a grand plan, but the problem was that you had to keep going. You had to keep yourself at that point of believing in it because if you didn't carry it through to the best of your ability, then you really didn't have a chance.

As she swam across, she wondered why she was doing this. It couldn't have been Craig. Anna was right; he was gone. He was working for someone else. Could she really get him back out? She doubted it.

She'd had to leave the UK. She'd had to leave his side, his facility, to understand this truth back in the cold, harsh world of the Service. She'd been told it by Justin and Anna. Maybe now she was actually doing it. Maybe this was all about her country. That's what she told herself as she swam over.

The two women arrived at the stanchions, which stood deep in the water, and slowly climbed up. They could hear people at the sides of the bridge. As they climbed over the railing, they could see that the bridge was empty, except for one man and a van. They leaped over the fence, stepped out into the middle of the road, and walked forward. Anna was at the front, Kirsten, three steps behind.

Kirsten looked around her. There were cars at the far end of the bridge, but they didn't look like the cars of normal people. They must have been Morozov's men. He'd expected her to route in from either end of the bridge. At one end, the cars were parked apart, creating a narrow lane. But at the other end, they were face-to-face with the women.

'Lie down on the floor,' said Morozov. The van doors opened and men with machine guns stepped out. Anna ignored them and kept walking forward.

'I said, "Lie down on the floor". We need to check if you're armed.'

'Of course, I'm armed,' said Anna. 'You asked me out here in the open and you think I'm not armed? We're armed. She is going to help me here,' she said.

'Then you come up from the water. That's not what you said. You don't even have a gun on you.'

'No,' said Anna. 'I don't, neither does she. We've got something much bigger trained on here.'

Morozov glared at her.

69

'You're lying,' he said.

'No, I'm not lying. I'm well trained and I'm not stupid. Anything happens to me and this bridge blows.'

'You couldn't bring equipment like that to this city without my knowledge,' he said.

'Of course, I could,' she said. 'It's not difficult. Your people would've done it in other places around the globe. Shall we cut out the nonsense and talk?'

'Olev said you wanted to talk about Gethsemane. Why do you want to talk about Gethsemane?'

'Because I need to get to know her better. She's currently in the UK,' said Anna. 'You're probably aware of that. I want to know more about her. Have you sent her there on a job?'

The man didn't flinch. He was standing in a long coat. There were no visible weapons on him, and he calmly stepped forward towards Anna. 'You look soaked and very vulnerable out here.'

'I'm anything but vulnerable,' said Anna. 'Do you know who I am?'

The man looked at her.

'You don't, do you? Maria, you're wondering who Maria is. You should have scanned my face by now. Are they running the recognition? I hope they're running the recognition. When you know who I am, you'll make sure this is a civilised conversation.'

'You must be desperate,' he said. 'Desperate to know about her.'

'You could say that,' retorted Anna.

'Desperate people make mistakes; desperate people do silly things. Have you done a silly thing here?'

'You tell me,' said Anna. 'I want information. I want to know about her. She's freelance, isn't she?'

The man raised his eyebrows slightly, giving away the answer, but then said, 'No.'

'Freelance for whom?' asked Anna. 'Working for you quite closely.'

She could see the earpiece when someone said something in the Morozov's ear because the man actually cocked his head towards it. It was funny, but it was probably because of the wind. If you didn't hear something and it came from that side, you would turn your head towards it. Of course, it wasn't coming from that side; it was coming from the earpiece, but people have habits. That was one of his. It told Anna something.

Behind Anna, Kirsten was scanning the bridge. In front, there were cars and there was no way off behind. More cars blocked the road. If the man would not come willingly, they were going off the bridge. It was a significant drop, but done properly, it wouldn't be that difficult to enter the water safely. Morozov would be the problem.

He wouldn't dive off the bridge. He wouldn't jump with his feet perfectly together. Instead, he would have to be dragged off the bridge and if he smacked his head on the way down, that could be dangerous. A definite risk.

This was a big prize in a dangerous move by Anna. Kirsten was partly against it, but she didn't have another plan. Kirsten stared at Morozov, and one thing that was bothering her was the way he was looking at Anna Hunt. She'd seen the cocking of the head and guessed that he must know it was Anna by now.

At higher levels, Anna Hunt was a legend, and she was a legend in Russia. To bring Anna Hunt in, to capture her, the man would become a legend in his own right. And what could they get from her? So much detail, so much hidden away, and she'd walked bare-faced up to them and stood right in front of him. No gun. Nothing to threaten him with.

Kirsten was finding it difficult because she couldn't understand any of the conversation. Anna had told her not to worry about that. Kirsten's job was to time the exit, get it right. She watched the conversation going back and forth. It was becoming more heated. Much more heated. Two of the men from the van behind Morozov were coming forward. The weapons were low, pointed to the ground, but Kirsten could see trigger hands were flexing ever so slightly.

He's going to go for this, she thought, *going to go for the grab. He knows it's Anna Hunt. The prize is before him and he knows what she's worth.*

She watched for Morozov's hands closely. One was inside the coat. The other, his right hand, was outside. The right hand never flinched, but the left came out from the coat.

Kirsten looked up, watching the men with the guns, and saw the movement. She stepped forward, right arm swinging out, knife into hand and then releasing. Then her left foot forward and the left hand coming out, knife releasing. The two members beside Morozov were hit on the neck and gurgled, guns dropping to the ground.

Before Morozov could react, Kirsten stepped forward, tapped Anna on the back, and ran for the side of the bridge. It took her about three seconds to get there. She jumped up, one foot onto the railing, and then dived out into the dark below.

Anna stepped forward once Kirsten had tapped her. She tried to grab Morozov, but saw a man with a gun stepping out of the van. There wasn't time. She wouldn't have time to get him. Anna turned, followed Kirsten up onto the railing and straight down to the water.

Kirsten had her hands out in front of her, executing an excellent dive into the water. The cold raced back up over her, but standing on the bridge, she'd felt the chill, anyway. Justin would be on the move. She stayed low, swimming as hard as she could underneath the surface.

She heard gunfire. Now the water was dark, and she struggled to see, but she reckoned she was going in the correct direction. She swam on and on until she had to lift her head above the surface. Her ears heard the gunfire, and she was back down.

Kirsten didn't wait for Anna. Anna would have to take care of herself, and she hoped she was behind her. She came up for a breath of air the next time and a hand tapped her on the head. Kirsten reached up, felt the side of the boat, pulled, and rolled herself in. She got up on her knees as gunfire was in the surrounding water. Anna was there, and she pulled her in too. Then there was a yell.

Justin was clutching his leg, screaming. Kirsten grabbed the motor of the boat, turned and opened up the throttle as best she could, racing it towards a far bank. They'd have to be expeditious. The car wasn't that far away, but they needed to get out of the area before they were cornered off.

The location of the car meant it would take Morozov's people at least five minutes to get from the bridge to where they got out onto the bank. As the boat ran up to the bank, Anna jumped out, held it tight as Kirsten threw Justin's arm around her neck. He was bleeding badly, but there was no time to apply a tourniquet yet. They'd do that in the car.

The car was two streets away. At first Justin limped along,

but Kirsten stopped him, turned, put her shoulder into his ribs, and threw him over it. She carried him as Anna ran ahead down the streets past a rather bemused tramp. Once Anna reached the car, she threw the rear door open.

Kirsten threw Justin into the back. Anna took the keys off Justin, started the car up, and told Kirsten to get into the rear with him. Justin had his leg up. Kirsten then pulled his trouser back as hard as she could. She examined the wound; the blood was pouring but there was no exit wound.

'It's still in there,' she said to Anna, 'bullet in deep. I can't get it with anything.'

'Wrap it up,' said Anna, as the car flew off around the corner. 'Wrap it up and get your heads down.'

Kirsten ripped part of Justin's trouser leg and tied it tight around the wound, hopefully, to stop the bleeding. She lay down, pressing Justin into the seat. She could hear him whimper. The man was in serious pain.

'Where do we go?' asked Kirsten from the back.

'Shut the hell up,' said Anna. 'I need to get us out of here first.'

The car crashed hard into something, and Kirsten was thrown against the seats in the front. She fell down into the well behind the front seats.

'What the hell was that?'

'Somebody trying to take us off the road. Shut up.'

Kirsten tried to clamber up and threw herself into the front seat. As Anna continued to drive erratically, Kirsten reached down into the well of the car, picked up a handgun left previously, and rolled down the window. Someone was coming head-on towards them.

Anna whipped the car to the side and Kirsten fired several

shots at the tires of the oncoming car, followed by several through the windscreen. Glass erupted. The car narrowly missed them, careering off behind them into a wall.

Anna turned left down a road, down another two streets, and then into the back of a complex. It was a rundown part of town, but the spare car was there. They'd prepped it for the escape, hoping they wouldn't have to come back and find it. Now they'd have to be quick.

Kirsten jumped out of the car as Anna pulled it to a halt beside her new one. She helped Justin out into that car and Anna drove away quickly with no headlights on. She followed a small river down what wasn't a road but a track. The track came out through a gate and onto a main road.

Anna drove quickly, but steadily. A few cars passed by, but none reacted to her, and soon, they were back at their flat. Kirsten helped Justin out of the car, noting that the blood was no longer running from his leg. This was good, and they kept it fairly clean going up the steps into the flat. Once inside, Anna rushed out, quickly scrubbing off any traces of blood that may have been left behind.

Justin was lying on the couch, his leg elevated. It didn't look good. He needed help. It would just get worse if that bullet wasn't removed, but here they were in the middle of Saint Petersburg. There was no evacuation coming. There was no Service that you could call in. During normal times, it would have been difficult from this position, never mind what the current state of the Service was. Anna marched into the room.

'He needs a doctor,' said Kirsten.

Anna sat down, staring over at her. 'Okay,' she said. 'Time to find him a doctor.' Then she turned and kicked the table. 'Dammit,' she said. 'Didn't have time to grab him. Dammit.'

Chapter 10

Anna Hunt paced the flat. Her mind focused somewhere in the deep recesses of her mind, pulling in past contacts. It was like a filing system, bringing ideas to mind, then shuffling them out of the way. Justin would need a doctor, someone to at least get this bullet out, and he would need them fast. Meanwhile, the FSB would have St. Petersburg crawling with their men. How to keep everything quiet, how to be under the radar with all this heat going on? But if she didn't, Justin's wound could get infected and he could die.

Kirsten kept staring at Anna Hunt, and it was getting on Anna's nerves. *What did the woman expect? We're looking for a miracle at the moment, as if I could just magic up ideas.*

The bridge had been a bad idea. They'd been overzealous, overplayed it, and for what? But they needed more on Gethsemane. That's why they'd come here, to get to the root cause of what was happening. Was it a Russian plot? Was it revenge? What was going on at home? Why was Godfrey such a focus?

The story was that he'd left her, but that didn't explain bringing the Service down. That required more, and Anna hadn't been satisfied. But trying to satisfy that curiosity may have ended up seriously injuring Justin, if not worse. He had a fever running. He was in pain, but he was hanging on as best he could. There was the blood loss, and yes, he would need a transfusion, probably. A lot of rest too, but for the moment, they needed to get that bullet out.

Then it came to her; Sergei. Sergei might do it. He had fancied Anna back in the day. She'd only been a young thing then, and she had led him on, led him on to get into the underbelly of the gangster society. He was still here. He wasn't a gang lord on the level of Artyom and Orlov. Sergei was low-level, but he had a club, or at least he previously owned a club. She turned around, looking at Kirsten.

'I think I've got it,' she said, 'Sergei. It's risky, but I don't think we have any other choice. By the time we organise an extraction and get out of here, it might be too late for Justin. It might be too late for the leg.'

'What do you want me to do?' asked Kirsten.

'Stay here. Stay here until I see Sergei. It won't take me more than a couple of hours if his club still exists, and he's still running it. Last I heard, he was still here. Always low level, never much more, but he liked me back in the day, had a real thing for me. We'll see if the old memories are enough.'

Anna Hunt had changed, now wearing a leather jacket, black trousers, and boots. She went armed this time, and Kirsten wondered if she should stay close, but Anna said Justin needed her. That was true. Kirsten kept mopping his forehead, a fever running through him. At times, he was delirious. Other times, he seemed to understand his own situation.

It was five in the morning when Anna got back. She shut the door behind her, checked the windows, and then turned to Kirsten.

'We're in luck, but we're going to have to move quick. Preferably before sun up. He's got a second club these days, and in the rear, there won't be much happening today. He said if we can get Justin in there, he'll get a doctor to us.'

'Do you trust him?' asked Kirsten.

'We've no option,' she said, 'but he looked at me the way he used to. Those eyes, he wanted to own me back in the day.'

'I can't imagine that ended well for him.'

'No,' said Anna. 'I broke his heart, and now I've just walked back into his life. I don't know how he'll play it overall.'

'Well, let's get Justin on the move then, before the sun comes up, proper.'

The pair of them took Justin Chivers down and into the car. He was laid down in the backseat. The two women, taking up the front seats, listened to him moan as they drove around St. Petersburg until they found the club that Sergei had told Anna about. She drove into the rear yard, parked the car, and then knocked at the door.

It was opened by a large man with short hair who took one look at Anna, then the car, and ushered them inside. Justin was carried through by Kirsten, and then a table was shown where she was to dump him. She laid him down carefully, looked around, and found a cushion to put underneath his head. The large man said something to Anna in Russian.

'He says, "The doctor's on his way, as is Sergei." I best get ready.'

'Ready for what?' asked Kirsten.

Anna took off her jacket and brushed her hair. 'I'm needing to keep this guy sweet because we're getting Justin fixed, and then we're getting out of here. I don't intend to hang around, but while he's here, I'll keep him entertained.'

It was ten minutes before Sergei burst into the room. He made a beeline straight for Anna Hunt, who embraced him, wrapping her arms around him and kissing him on the lips. She let him keep his arm around her. As he turned to face Kirsten, he said something to her in Russian.

'You'll need to speak English to this one,' said Anna, 'and I'm not sure if she would've taken that as a compliment.'

'Why not?' he asked. 'How do you translate it?'

'Daughter of the mayor,' said Anna, 'At least the first bit. I'm not translating what you said afterwards.'

'Why not?' asked Kirsten.

'Because it's what he would like to do to you,' said Anna, 'and it was incredibly vulgar.' The man smiled, stared over at Kirsten, eyeing her up and down.

'Definitely a daughter of the mayor, though.'

'Where's the doctor?' asked Kirsten.

'She's like you as well. I'm surprised you haven't asked before,' said Sergei. 'He's just outside. The boys are frisking him down.'

An older man entered the room carrying a black bag. Behind him, one of Sergei's contingent carried several bags. The man opened them up, and Kirsten peered inside to find bags of blood.

'In case he needs a transfusion. Now, back out of the way,' said the man.

He took the crude bandages off Justin's leg, investigated the wound, and checked Justin's temperature. The man prepared an injection, gave it to Justin, and then began taking tools out.

'I'll need you to hold him steady. I can get the bullet out. Best if he doesn't walk on the leg, get him some kind of crutch. I can stabilise it, but you'll need to take him to a proper hospital, eventually. I take it you can't do that in St. Petersburg. That's why you're here with me. I don't need to know why,' said the doctor. 'However, I will need paid,' he said to Sergei.

Sergei said something back, and Anna whispered to Kirsten. He told him, 'You'll get paid in good time.'

The women held Justin down, while the doctor worked on his leg. There was the occasional flinch, but Justin looked as if he'd been knocked out to a large degree. It took a while, but eventually, the bullet was removed, and the doctor put fresh bandages around the leg, strapping it up tight. It was left elevated, and the doctor then performed a blood transfusion.

By the time the doctor left, satisfied that this patient would at least be on the mend if not completely healed, it was getting after five o'clock in the evening. Sergei invited the women through into his club for something to eat.

Kirsten followed Anna, who sat down beside Sergei and started tucking into the Chinese food that had been provided.

'Probably more to your Western tastes,' said Sergei, 'than what we normally would provide.'

Kirsten and Anna ate hungrily, but looked around and identified the interior of a strip club.

'Making money and looking at women,' said Sergei. 'It's what I like to do. Why wouldn't I want to own one of these places? I was always disappointed that you never worked here,' he said to Anna. 'Your friend would look good, too. I treat my girls well. They're protected, looked after, and you can't say that about everywhere in this city. I'm a businessman. They make my clients happy; they gain their rewards.'

'I'm sure they do,' said Kirsten.

A woman walked past in tight jeans and a half-cut top. Sergei jumped up, wrapped his arms around her.

'Francesca here—she's happy here, aren't you?'

The woman gave a faint smile. Kirsten looked at her and wondered what age the girl was. *Be lucky if she was eighteen,* she thought.

They finished their food as several girls came in and began doing dance routines up on the stage. They were clothed, at least to a dancer's standard, with leggings and some form of leotard or top on. But the dances they performed were definitely of the erotic sort.

'You can stay with me tonight here,' said Sergei. 'I've got a suite upstairs. I'm quite happy to stay with you and protect you,' he said.

'When have I ever needed protecting?' asked Anna. 'But I might stay with you. Might be a good place to hide out.'

One of the larger men came over and whispered something in Sergei's ear.

'You're certainly causing a stir around town,' said Sergei. 'They're looking for you. They might come in here tonight, but they won't come to the back rooms. I doubt they know you were in contact with me, and anyway, it was twenty years ago.'

'How much did you pay the doctor?' asked Anna. 'The going rate or more?'

'He does lots of jobs for me, so he got the going rate. He knows he'll be back for more. Don't worry; he won't betray us.'

'The FSB are likely to put a large amount on my head. Kirsten here, they'll want her too.'

Sergei stared at them both. 'Then I'll have to hide you both. Your friend, too. Hopefully, he'll be waking up soon.'

'I'm not sure that I'm happy staying here, Sergei,' said Anna. 'I appreciate your help. I really do. Have you somewhere else we could stop? Somewhere else only you know about. If I felt safer . . .' said Anna. She reached round behind Sergei's neck and rubbed it. 'I could—well, we could have a much more friendly night. I'd be less on the lookout, less worried about what was going to happen.'

'If anyone comes, this is the place we should be,' said Sergei. 'You stay here and I can defend you here.'

Anna ran her hand behind his neck again, reached over, kissed him on the lips, then stepped back, saying she was just going to check on Justin in the back room. Kirsten had finished her food and followed her, giving Sergei a nod. As she entered the rear room, she could see Justin was conscious, and looking around him.

'We're not staying here,' said Anna. 'Sergei gets a little inflated about his own success. The idea he could protect us here, if the FSB came in. They'd rip the place apart, destroy him. If he had any brains on his shoulders, he'd take me up on my offer, take us away somewhere. But as he's not, we're going to need to move.'

'Are you up to it, Justin?' asked Kirsten.

'God knows,' said Justin. 'The moment the room's still, we'll get on the move.'

Kirsten helped him to sit up, but he put both arms down, holding onto the table.

The double doors into the room burst open and Sergei came in with the large man who had first greeted them when they arrived at the club.

'Andre will stay here,' he said. 'They're coming in the front. I will deal with them. I will send them away. Do not worry.'

Sergei turned, exited through the doors, and Andre closed them behind him. Kirsten looked around. There was no other exit from the room. She looked over at Anna, who shook her head. Kirsten reached for Justin, putting an arm around her neck and helping him up onto his feet. He was leaning on her, clinging to her in some ways, incredibly unstable, but at least he was conscious. He was contributing something towards their movement.

There came gunfire from outside the room. Kirsten reckoned it was from the front of the building. Not that close yet.

'Go get Justin in the car. Go,' said Anna.

'No, no, you stay. You stay,' said Andre. 'I am told you have to stay.'

Anna delivered one punch to him, knocking the man into the wall. He tumbled to the floor. Anna opened the doors and helped Kirsten carry Justin through. She looked down the corridor, saw somebody peeking out, and realised it wasn't one of the club's workers. Instead, it was the FSB. A gun was raised towards her, but Anna dispatched the man with two quick shots.

'Go, down that corridor, out through the back. It's the only chance. We need to get Justin in the car. You'll never make it away on foot.'

Kirsten turned, dropped her shoulder, picked Justin up, and ran down the corridor. Behind her, she heard Anna Hunt firing several times.

'We'll wait for you,' said Kirsten.

'Don't you dare. See you back at the flat,' she said. 'Rendezvous at the flat!'

Kirsten ran, kicked open the double doors at the rear of the club. She was carrying her weapon in her right hand, Justin over her left shoulder. As she reached the car, two men came in from the back gate, and she threw Justin onto the bonnet. She fired quickly, two shots, hitting each of them, sending them sprawling on the ground.

They weren't clean shots. They weren't shots that would kill them, but it would keep them occupied on the ground. She turned back, rolled Justin onto her shoulder, opened the back door of the car and practically threw him inside.

Kirsten stood up, checked the perimeter, saw another two men coming, and fired at them both. She then jumped inside the car, took out the keys and drove off. Another man stepped through the gate, and she rammed him, sending him over the top of the car.

As she reached the road, cars screamed after her, and Kirsten was in a panic. Where could she go? She tried to focus on her route as she took a left, a left, and a right, and then headed down an alley, stopping where it reached the crossroads of alleys.

She pulled on the brake and noticed that the car behind her had slowed down. Part of the alley had narrowed across, and while her car was small, the FSB car was wide and couldn't get through. She got out of the car, opened the back door, picked Justin up onto her shoulder, and started running down the new alleyway. She took a cutting into the right, then went on through a house, coming out the front.

There was a motorbike waiting outside. She got Justin to sit upright, placing him where the main rider would normally be. She jumped the bike, getting it to start. Before getting round behind Justin, she pushed him forward so his head was resting on the fuel tank and she rode off.

She wasn't about to leave Anna in a hurry though, worried that the number of FSB around would've caused her a problem. She tore along the street on the bike. From along the street, she stopped, looking down to where the premises of the club were. At the rear gates, she saw someone being led out. Kirsten recognised the black attire. She recognised the frame of Anna Hunt from a distance. She looked battered, bruised, and most definitely, was in FSB custody.

Chapter 11

J ustin and Kirsten made it back to the flat, where Kirsten helped him up to lie down on the sofa before she disappeared to hide the bike some distance away. People may have seen them riding along with his head down on the main body of the bike, clearly not in a condition to be transported. While it wasn't a reason to say they were spies, it was something unusual to report. The bike may then get checked if it was parked outside the building. Anything that would lead to them had to be put out of the way.

Kirsten picked up some food from a local shop before returning to the flat. She had learned a few words in Russian, basic 'thanks', nothing more, but it was enough to get her by. She also shopped some distance away from where they were staying. When she got back, she made some food and got Justin to eat. He was exhausted, a little disorientated, and Kirsten took some time to tell him what had happened.

'We can't leave her,' said Kirsten. 'One thing we can't do is leave her behind. I need to get her.'

'It's a risky mission, foolhardy,' said Justin. 'They'll have her at the local FSB headquarters. If she's in there, you'll not be able to break in. To go in and shoot your way out, you'll have more than the Saint Petersburg branch on you. You'll create a major incident. They will guard her and guard her well. They'll also be feeding it back. Moscow will get hold of it. They'll want her,' said Justin.

'It looked like she took a beating,' said Kirsten. 'She took a beating to get us out of there. She took a risk getting you there to get you treated.'

'Yes, she did,' said Justin. 'Forgive me, because I'm the one drugged up. I'm the one who's woozy, but she did it for a purpose and she succeeded in that purpose of getting me the treatment. Your purpose would be to get her out and you won't succeed by doing it this way.'

'I've broken into places before,' said Kirsten.

'Yes, you have, but not places like this. Olev Volkof was nothing. He had a secret office outside the main reaches of the FSB. You're talking about trying to break into the lion's den. They do guard these places openly, and they're very capable at it. It's not like trying to hide the place where you work. This is the FSB headquarters; they know she's in there. They've taken her there because it is the most guarded. It's not the time.'

Kirsten turned away in frustration. Of course, Justin was right. Of course, he was right, but she had to try.

'Are you able to do anything?' she asked him.

He tried to stand up on his foot, but it was too painful. The doctor had left him painkillers, and he was taking them, but they were making him woozy. 'I'm telling you—we wait this one out.'

'We can't do that. I have to keep eyes on the building.'

'That's what they'll be looking for. They'll be looking for you, watching. Maybe we should try to contact the Americans. They might help us. They won't have associated them with us yet. If we can get them to watch the building and report back to us.'

'No, no,' said Kirsten. 'We went into this to go dark. We haven't looked for help from anyone except for people who aren't associated with us. Maybe I'll drop by Sergei.'

'That would be a good place to start, but there's nothing to say they won't have taken him away, especially if they were shooting at him. After all, they shot at Anna. They'll see him as harbouring us.'

'It's worth a look. I'll be careful,' said Kirsten. 'I know how to be careful.'

Kirsten left Justin with enough food and drink to keep him going and walked to where she'd hidden the motorbike. It was still in amongst the undergrowth of a small park and she rode towards the club they'd been in. As she passed it by, she saw many women standing outside, waiting to get in.

Kirsten took the bike round to another street, parked it, and took off her jacket, leaving it over the bike. She took her T-shirt and, tying a knot in it, made it sit up much higher on her. Her leggings would serve a purpose. Kirsten wanted to look as tramp-like as possible, a girl who would work in here.

When she turned up, she saw the stares of the other girls. Words were said in Russian, but she ignored them and then watched the two front doors open. She recognised the doorman, who Anna had slugged previously. The girls filed into the club. Doors were closed behind them, but they continued down towards some changing areas. Kirsten had held her ground, and turned to the man who had opened the doors, approaching him as soon as he locked them behind him.

'You speak English, don't you?' said Kirsten.

The man looked left and right, almost fearful when he saw

who it was.

'They took her,' he said. 'They took her and they took Sergei as well. The FSB told me I had to open up as normal, told me I had to make it look like we were still working, in case you came back. They reckoned you'll be here. They've been watching. Some of those girls are not ours.'

'The FSB took Sergei away?' queried Kirsten. 'Is he still there? Where do you think they've held him?'

'They brought him back,' said the man. 'He's in the back room, but unlike your man, he'll not recover.'

So, Sergei was dead. That option was out. Kirsten saw a man she didn't recognise coming along the corridor. She reached up, grabbed the back of the head of the large man in front of her, and kissed him on the lips. She took his hand, slapped it onto her backside and squirmed in his grasp like she was enjoying it. The man walked past, and then Kirsten broke off.

'I'm a danger to you,' she said. 'I'm going now. Open these doors again. I won't come back.'

The man nodded, opened the door, and closed it behind him. Kirsten undid the tie on her T-shirt and it dropped. She walked back to her motorbike. She threw the jacket on and soon disappeared, her hair feathering out in the breeze.

The local FSB HQ was easily identifiable and when they had earlier looked at getting Anna Hunt back in their flat, Justin had shown the location to her. She parked the bike a distance away and walked a path close to it. There were flats around the building, a restaurant down below. Kirsten saw a man of maybe sixty entering a flat above the restaurant. She followed him up, opening her jacket, taking it down off her shoulders.

'You want?' she said.

The man stared at her. She lifted her T-shirt up, standing

in her bra. She put her hand out, rubbing her thumb and finger together, showing she wanted money. The man nodded, opened the door for her, and she stepped inside. He closed it behind himself. He locked it and turned round to find himself picked up by the throat. His head bounced off the wall. He collapsed on the ground.

She took him to the bedroom of his flat. Kirsten searched the flat, found some rope, bound and gagged him. She crept to the window at the front, pulled up a chair, and observed the front of the building. Kirsten sent Justin a message. She coded it and never said where she was, but advised him she was watching the FSB Building. He should be ready to be on the move soon as Anna would be taken somewhere and possibly before nightfall.

Kirsten sat there for the evening, only disappearing into the kitchen of the flat to get some food to eat. By the time it got to midnight, there was no sign of Anna Hunt being removed from the building. So, Kirsten decided she would look around it.

There was a large fence around the rear, which would be high to scale. There was a lower fence over to the west side of the compound. Kirsten approached this from down an alleyway. There were guards walking round, and they certainly seemed to enter this bit.

Walking past, she quickly jumped up, grabbed onto the mesh fence and scampered up it. Reaching the top, she put her foot in where there was barbed wire, but was able to jump off it and land, albeit with a slight bit of pain in her right ankle on hitting the ground. She removed her gun from inside her jacket. The silencer was on it.

She stared at her surroundings. There was a long passage to

the right side of the compound she stood in. The passage ran down the side of the building. Kirsten wondered why it was there. It had a mesh top and she would have to crawl along it. It was wide enough for maybe two of her. Height-wise, it would barely reach her waist. Other than that, it led into this compound.

She noticed there was a gate, which was electronic. That could shut off the access to the corridor down the side of the building. Kirsten was bemused, but it looked like a route in.

She got down on her knees, slowly making her way forward. As she got halfway down, she could hear a faint growl. Then there was a slight whimper. Kirsten understood where she was. This was a dog run. This was the way they let them out so they could run around in the back.

As she looked up ahead in the dark, she could see off to one side a weak light and a small door. It was more of a hatch. The hatch slid up, and a dog wandered out, sniffing the air. She realised the wind was behind her. For a moment, the dog turned to stare at her.

Kirsten didn't hesitate about shooting the dog. It fell over with a whimper. Kirsten wasn't sure how you tagged the dog to make sure it didn't make a sound. Humans were different. They didn't teach you how to kill dogs quietly.

What bothered her, as she started backtracking along the little corridor, was the sound of paws coming out of that hole. She was nearly at the end of the corridor when several dogs rushed her. They barked. She continued to backtrack as she fired, a couple of dogs going down, but others fighting to get past. She had blocked them, but not for long as they fought past the bodies.

Kirsten felt herself go clear of the corridor. She reached forward, pulled the gate that would normally be on an automatic spring shut. A couple of dogs barrelled into it. She turned round and leapt to the fence. Kirsten heard a whir as the door opened again. Dogs ran out, jumped, and she whipped her feet away as a set of nasty teeth went rushing past. She kept climbing.

Hearing a shot, she threw herself off the top of the fence. They would come now. Come for her, believing she would run away. Instead, Kirsten turned and ran to the flat.

She kept to the shadows, grateful to reach the flat door and step inside, just as the FSB poured out of their own headquarters. She ran up to the door of the flat, up above the restaurant, and let herself in. Kirsten locked it behind her. She sat close to the window, but back from it, so they couldn't see her.

The hunt in the street quickly fanned out further, and it would be four hours before everyone returned. She did not know if Anna Hunt was still there. Kirsten would have to watch, have to continue to be patient.

She looked down in the street and saw the dogs being paraded. They would be sniffing. Where had she gone? If they came towards the flat, she would leave. She'd go out the back somewhere, take to a window. At the moment, the dogs didn't seem to be on her trail. Maybe they hadn't got a good enough whiff. Maybe the ones that had were dead. Who knew? Either way, Kirsten kept herself hidden inside the flat.

She messaged Justin. Briefly explaining what she'd done, but saying that Anna wasn't on the move.

The waiting was always the hardest part for Kirsten. She felt the tiredness, but she couldn't go into that sentry sleep because she needed to keep her eyes open. If there were any departures from the headquarters, she needed to know.

Kirsten felt herself nodding off. She would pinch herself. She would prod herself, make sure she stayed awake. This was Anna, after all. If they got Anna away from here, she wouldn't be coming back.

Kirsten disappeared for a drink of water and to wash her face. When she returned, she saw a large van. It was like one of those prison vans at home. High, narrow windows, so you couldn't see in. This would be it. On the move. Would it be for Anna?

The van was there for an hour and then it drove out with a car in front of it and a car behind. Kirsten looked carefully. The cars were full. A proper escort. This had to be it.

Maybe they were doing a dummy run to flush her out, but this was Anna. She was worth the risk. Kirsten stood up quickly and made for the flat door. It was time to go back to work. All she had was a bike, a gun, and her quick wits. It would have to be enough.

Chapter 12

Kirsten raced down to find her bike several blocks away and tore off into the early morning traffic. St. Petersburg was like any city, with plenty on the move, and this slowed down the escorted van she was trying to tail. She wasn't sure where the best place to intercept it would be if she was in amongst the traffic. There would be all the chaos, even police units, and other FSB trying to get near them. It could cause a problem for them. However, the public was also milling about.

Kirsten was always one for avoiding civilian casualties, even at this dire time. She may have been on foreign soil, but there were certainly innocent people about. She waited to see the route taken by the van headed towards the south of St. Petersburg. But the van got stuck in early morning traffic.

Kirsten was on a motorbike capable of weaving in and out amongst the cars. Could she break Anna out of this position? Where would they go? They'd have to get clear on foot, get clear of this jam, but it would stop any extra FSB coming in. Unless they could somehow pull out a helicopter, this could be an excellent chance. She'd be up against only those in the escort.

Kirsten rode up between cars, getting closer and closer, but then realised it wasn't a two-car escort. There was another one behind. She could tell because a man was watching her in the rearview mirror all the way up as she shot between the traffic.

She rode up, stopped, and tapped his window, indicating he needed to move the car to the left to let her past. He looked up at her once, twice. He wound the window down and by the time he looked a third time, she'd shot him in the head and also the man sitting across from him.

She jumped off the bike, and started shooting the car in front through the rear screen window. One man got out, and she tagged him as well as she routed closer towards the van. The car in front now opened up, as four men routed back towards the van, but Kirsten had jumped from the car onto the back door of the van, pulling herself up onto the roof. She ran to one side and shot the man coming towards her before he'd even got close.

Those on the other side may have heard the click of a shot, so Kirsten went flat on the roof, and crawled over to the edge. She saw them there waiting, prepped to shoot up at her, so she rolled to the rear of the van, dropped onto the bottom of the car. They must have heard her land and came running around the corner to be shot by her. In the space of thirty seconds, she'd taken out everyone in the accompanying cars.

There were lots of screaming, a myriad of panicked people, some opening doors and running away from the scene. Others locked car doors, ducking down, but Kirsten needed to get inside the van.

It was trying to move now, pushing the car in front, driving backwards and forwards, shunting anything in its way. Kirsten would have to be careful not to get caught in between it and any of the other cars. She gave a wide berth.

Instead, she walked down low behind the cars to the side of the van. As she got towards the front wheel of one car, she realised she was in line with where the driver would be in the van's front. She stood up, identified him, shot him.

The far door of the van opened, but Kirsten ran up, got into the front driver's seat by pulling the man out. She saw that the other man was down low, round the front of the van. He hadn't clocked that she'd gone up into it.

Kirsten started the van. The man stood up looking panicked, went to shoot at her and blew out the front windscreen as she ducked down low. But she drove the accelerator forward, and the van rammed him up against the car. Other cars were panicked now, and started pushing, but Kirsten needed to get off this main road. Needed to get somewhere else with the van.

She turned the wheel, driving it forward, ramming a car. Then she reversed back, ramming into the other car, turning the wheel again. There was a side street off to the left if she could get there. Cars were funnelling into it now, desperate to get away from the scene. Sirens were wailing to the sky. People were coming, and she needed to get away.

Kirsten was, of course, in a highly identifiable van. She'd also need to open up the doors. She knew she couldn't see anything from opening the doors up inside the van. However, she continued back and forward, ramming cars front and left. They gradually moved aside, drove off as quick as they could, and she had a clear route to the side alley. As she drove into it, the wing mirrors of the van were clipped off, and she knocked several cats of the alley out of the way.

Kirsten wanted to turn right, but she couldn't and had to wait until the alley came out into another large road. She spun the vehicle left, overran up onto the pavement, knocking people out of the way. There was no time to hesitate. She couldn't worry about them. They may have been innocent, but what was she to do? She had to get Anna Hunt out of there.

The street she had driven into at least had flowing traffic, a lot of it moving out of her way, on realising that something was wrong. Anna was in the back of the vehicle, no doubt being thrown about, but there were people in there with her. Kirsten needed to get her out quick. In this van, she was easily identifiable.

She was in a foreign city and didn't know where she was going. Anna Hunt knew St. Petersburg, or at least, the St. Petersburg of old. She could understand where to run, how to run. Kirsten saw a large building up ahead. Its walls looked solid and it had a sharp point where the two sides of the building met.

She drove up and spun the vehicle around, and it slid with its rear doors pointing at the building. From ten metres away, Kirsten put the van in reverse and drove as hard as she could into the wall. There was a sickening thud, a crash. Her airbag exploded, and she ignored it, putting the vehicle into a forward gear and driving forward. She then reversed again heavily, hearing another crash.

Once more she pulled forward, but this time, she stopped, putting the handbrake on, jumped out of the vehicle, and ran around to the rear. The door was smashed in. There was a gap and inside was a mess of bodies.

Kirsten stepped up to the gap, looked inside, and saw someone on the floor. He clearly wasn't Anna Hunt, and she shot him. She stepped in further, saw another man at the rear, dazed and confused, and then two seconds later, he was dead. Anna was handcuffed and lying in the middle of the floor.

'Get up,' said Kirsten. 'We need to get out of here.'

Anna looked up. *The woman's head must be ringing*, thought Kirsten, feeling the effects of the crash despite having instigated it. 'Come on,' she said, grabbing Anna's wrists and pulling her up to her feet.

Kirsten stepped out through the small gap of the bashed in door and heard cars screeching down the road. She reached back, helped Anna through, and tore off into a nearby shop. It was a bakery, and she ran through to the back, knocking bread rolls to the floor. People dived out of the way, unsure of what was happening. Kirsten kicked out the rear door. She turned, saw Anna stumbling behind her, grabbed her hands and put the wrists up against the wall. She shot the handcuffs. Anna's hands moved to the side, and Kirsten grabbed one of her hands and dragged her along the street.

Clearly, the woman was groggy, and Kirsten didn't blame her for that, but cut left and right, running away as best as she could. Kirsten did not know where she was going, just away, away somewhere quiet, somewhere they could lie down. She burst into the door of a chocolatier, looked around and saw no customers. Kirsten turned and closed the door and saw a sign in Russian, flipping it over to its other side. She presumed it said 'Closed', and then pulled curtains across the door. She turned and held her gun, pointing it at the man behind the desk.

'You, where are the keys? Lock the door.'

The man looked at her, raising his hands, not understanding what she was saying. Anna mumbled something beside her in Russian. The man quickly shook his head, reached down, and threw Kirsten some keys. She handed Anna the gun, told her to point it at him, worked her way through the keys and eventually locked the door. She took the gun back off Anna, and they walked the man through to the rear of the shop. There were steps up and Kirsten made him follow them, and realised there was a flat upstairs where the man must live.

'Anyone else in the house? Anyone else likely to come to the house?'

The man was bemused. No idea what she was talking about. Anna mumbled something more at him. He mumbled something back in Russian.

'Lives on his own. Only shop. No one coming,' said Anna, her head swinging low. She clearly was groggier than Kirsten had realised.

Kirsten pushed the man down into a seat, pointed the gun at him, and told him to sit there. There was no translation needed as the man gripped the arms of the chair but didn't dare move.

'All around us,' said Kirsten to Anna. 'They're all around us.'

'Then we need to get out,' she said. 'We've got to get out of St. Petersburg. I need to know where we are,' she said. She turned to the man and said something in Russian. He said something back.

'We go south of here, out the back and take that road and keep going, take a right to to the outskirts of the city, then keep working south in that direction as far as we can. Get out into the country, regroup. Where's Justin?'

'Justin's woken up. I've left him in the flat.'

'Of course,' said Anna, 'Of course,' but she was puffing now, panting. The tension of the situation was washing over Kirsten.

She had an idea, but Anna probably wouldn't like it.

'Where do we stay?' asked Kirsten. 'Why don't we get back to the flat?'

'Because the FSB will be all over here. They'll be searching for us. out on the streets. They'll be everywhere.'

'We stick this man in a car from here. We make sure we're safe in that car. He drives off. We get out of the car. We tell him to keep going. They all go that way, we route back in.'

'But for what purpose? It's gone. We need to get away. Have to regroup outside. We need to go back to another country where we can heal up; see if it's still relevant.'

'Of course, it's relevant,' said Kirsten. 'You know we need more resolve. We need to know what he knows. It could change everything.'

'But we can't get him at the moment. We need to regroup.'

'There's isn't the time,' said Kirsten. 'Send this man off, get them chasing, and we double back, and we go for Morozov. We go for him at his home. We go for him when he isn't expecting us. He'll think that we've gone. He'll think that he's sent a manhunt after us.'

Anna Hunt bent forward from the chair she was sitting on, wheezing. It took her a moment to lift herself up onto her knees, pressing her elbows on her knees, steadying her head with her hands. She looked over at Kirsten.

'That is the craziest thing I have ever heard,' she said. 'You want, in the middle of all this, with the FSB all over us, to turn round and go after Morozov because you think they'll be misdirected in the hunting down this man.'

'Exactly, and if they go off after him, we can get Justin out as well. Justin can get himself out if he's able to move.'

'What do you mean, able to move? Is he, or isn't he?'

'Not really, but he'll have to,' said Kirsten. 'We go get Morozov, find out what we need, then we get clear, and we do it while this lot is on a manhunt for us.'

Anna Hunt started laughing. 'What's the matter?' asked Kirsten.

'That's the dumbest, craziest idea I've ever heard, and it just might work. It just might work,' said Anna.

Kirsten wasn't sure if the woman was short of air, and that was making her sound giddy. She stood up, walked over to Kirsten, and slapped her hand on her shoulder.

'The best of it is I'm going to tell this guy he's going to drive with the FSB on his back and we're going to have to convince him to do it. He's got no family, nobody else coming back here, and it all hinges on him keeping driving. I don't know how we do that.'

Kirsten looked around her. Was there something here he treasured? Was there something that we could threaten him with? There were no children, no wife. There were no girlfriends posted up on the wall. Every photo was just a picture of him outside this chocolate shop. Every photo was just him, smug with this bar of chocolate, that bar of chocolate. There were photos of him when he was much younger, maybe twenty, maybe thirty years ago.

There was one with an older man and *Yes*, thought Kirsten, *there's one with an older man with an older man again*. She looked up at Anna Hunt.

'Tell him we'll burn down this place. We will burn his chocolate shop to the ground if he doesn't help.'

Anna looked quizzically at Kirsten, and then she looked around to the photographs as well.

'You're evil,' she said. 'Totally evil. That's this man's baby,

101

isn't it? It's his all. That is genius,' she said.

She hobbled over, knelt down in front of the man who was shaking. He did not know what they were talking about, but he had the feeling that something would not be good. Anna Hunt, in the next two minutes, explained to the man exactly what was going to happen. She quizzed him on where his car was, quizzed him on how they could get clear, and then he would have to keep driving. The man nodded his head when she finished her explanation. He stood up and disappeared off.

'Where is he going?' asked Kirsten.

'He's off to change. He'll be five minutes and then he's going to take us. The man says that he'll do it gladly, and asked us not to hurt his little shop.'

'But we'll be with him. What's to stop him from giving us up?'

'The bomb in here. The bomb in here that I'm going to text him the code for once we're clear. Get on your knees and start putting a bomb in somewhere. Break the floorboard, make sure there's a hole he can see when he comes back.

'What are you on about?' asked Kirsten.

'He thinks I'm planting a bomb. Thinks I have the code for it. He thinks his shop is going to blow up.'

Kirsten laughed. 'You are devious,' she said. 'Devious.'

Anna Hunt bent over, her hands on her knees. 'And shattered,' she said. 'I'm shattered.'

For a moment, she looked like she was going to cry. Kirsten sensed something in her face, something that maybe Kirsten had seen before. Had she felt it before? She stared, but Anna Hunt smiled back.

'Time to go,' she said. 'Time to go. Just make sure you sort that bomb out.'

Chapter 13

Kirsten and Anna Hunt made their way back to the
FSB headquarters to sit it out and watch, waiting for
Morozov to leave the premises. They would tail him
back to his home under the premise that there would be less
security. Most of the men would still be chasing them out
of Saint Petersburg, following the trail the chocolatier was
setting.

They broke into another flat, bound and held its occupant,
and watched from the windows. As Anna sat in a chair, Kirsten
could see her agitation. Something had happened to her in that
headquarters, something bad. Anna being Anna was holding
it together, the consummate professional. But there were
tremors underneath, like an earthquake preparing to erupt.
These tremors were a warning. She could handle them. But
Kirsten was wondering when the real eruption would occur.

'I hope they haven't found the chocolatier yet,' said Anna.
'That'll scupper what we're doing. People will be back.'

'We might be in luck,' said Kirsten. 'Because if they find
the chocolatier, who knows, one, if they'll believe them.
Two, they'll start a search pattern from where they find him.

Hopefully, well outside Saint Petersburg.'

'I thought the bomb was a good idea,' said Anna. 'He went for it hook, line, and sinker.'

Kirsten grinned and watched as Anna gave a slight chuckle, but then that face came back. There was pain behind it. There was always pain in this job. Kirsten was aware of that. But this pain of Anna's was more personal, deep.

'Convoy on the move,' said Kirsten. 'Time to follow it.'

The two women quickly left the flat, but not before freeing the captive occupant's hands. Yes, he was terrified, but at least he'd be able to release himself now.

Down below in the street, Kirsten moved swiftly to a car she had targeted. While they were waiting, she would occasionally pop down to see what cars were available. Easy to steal. You needed one you could break into with no hassle. She found that car, Anna jumping into the seat beside her. The pair drove out into the traffic.

Morozov was in a BMW, different from most of the surrounding cars. And he wasn't that difficult to spot. His entourage, comprising at least three other cars, drove out of the city into the countryside. They made for a large building with a generous estate around it. Kirsten could see the high fences and guarded gates as she drove past, watching the entourage disappear off to the left and inside. The gates were firmly shut behind and Kirsten parked up a little distance away.

They were going in very light since the plan wasn't to be there for long. If they got into a major firefight, then they'd have blown it. The pair took a quick tour around the edge of the grounds.

It was heavily wooded and sported a large fence around the entire perimeter. However, like most large perimeters, it was difficult to maintain. Kirsten saw the odd camera, but she also thought she saw a blind spot. It was covered off by a guard post. She wondered how many should be there.

'Short of men,' said Anna. 'You'd have one stationed in that little hut and you'd have others patrolling, but they've only got the one patrolling. He really must have gone after us.'

'You think you can get up over that fence?' asked Kirsten.

'Quicker than you.'

The women watched the man performing sentry duties leave the little hut that was on a very plain lawn. Once over the fence, Anna could run without making much noise on the grass. She'd get herself to the guard post and then allow Kirsten to come over while covering her. Hopefully, she wouldn't need cover.

Anna ran forward, jumped up onto the fence as the guard was walking away. She clambered up, then slipped at the top, having to hang on desperately. The fence rattled. The guard stopped. He turned around, saw Anna at the top of it, and went to pull his gun. Anna was sure he was about to cry out as well.

But she saw the blood fly from the top of his head and he fell to the ground. She looked down and saw Kirsten at the fence, gun pointed through it. Anna breathed a sigh of relief, flung herself over the fence, and clambered down the other side before running to the guard post. Once there, she took up a squatting position, watching all around as Kirsten climbed the fence to join her.

'I thought you could handle that one.'

'Shut up,' said Anna. 'Do you know what age I am?'

Kirsten didn't. What would she put her as? The way she ran, how she could cut here and there, you would have said she was forty at most, maybe even mid-thirties. Anna was extremely fit, but the lines on her face, albeit an attractive face, would have said older.

'You can't keep the pace up forever,' said Anna. 'It doesn't work. Be aware of that.'

Kirsten nodded, and the two women peered out from the guard post, looking towards the main building. Night was falling and there were a few security spotlights, but the house wasn't lit up that well. Kirsten moved towards the dark, followed by Anna, and they edged along, moving towards a door. They spread on either side of the door as it was suddenly opened and a man in a chef's hat walked out.

He lit up a cigarette, unaware of the women on either side of him. As he stepped through, Anna stepped inside the door while Kirsten grabbed the man, hand over his mouth, dragging him back inside. Anna shut the door behind her and they looked around a small kitchen.

'Where's Morozov?' asked Anna in Russian.

The man said nothing but Kirsten throttled his neck. He would pass out eventually if she kept up this sort of pressure. Anna insisted on the question again.

'Where's Morozov?' The man said something back in Russian, croaking it out, struggling for breath.

'He said he fed him; he and the girl are upstairs.'

Kirsten looked at Anna. 'I thought he was married.'

'A lot of these are married,' said Anna. 'That's the downfall. They get a bit of power and they think they can have most women. In some places, it's still a perk of the job. I didn't climb the ladder thinking I could have whatever man I wanted. You?'

Kirsten went to say something back and then stopped.

'Sorry,' said Anna. 'Still feel raw?'

Kirsten nodded. She'd wanted Craig. She'd got Craig, and Craig was now gone, or at least she thought he was. If he had been dead, it might've been easier. Instead, he was in the middle of the operation she was fighting, possibly causing the Service to go down the tubes.

'No time to think about it now,' said Anna. 'He's upstairs with his bit of stuff. That's always good. They don't like too many guards around if they're entertaining. They'll be on the lower level. We need to put this guy somewhere, though.'

Kirsten kept the choke applied on the man, and shortly he passed out. She didn't kill him. Instead, they locked him in a cupboard in the kitchen, moving some of the stainless-steel furniture up against it to prevent him from coming out quickly. Together, the two women left the kitchen, stepping out into a large, luxurious hall.

The carpet looked expensive. The balustrade leading up to the top floor was immaculately cut wood. Together, running point for each other, they made their way to the top. There was one guard patrolling the upper floor. It was child's play waiting in the shadows and then to bring him down. Again, they knocked him out.

They could hear agitation from the room, and realised that the man had already started his nightly activities. Quickly, they opened the bedroom door.

Morozov was a large man, fat with white flesh that jiggled. He wasn't an appetising sight, but the woman beside him looked physically fit. From the look of her, Kirsten didn't think she was a woman of the night but someone else.

Anna pointed a gun, instructing Morozov in Russian to step back against the wall. She waved at the girl that was with him, telling her to go over to the other corner. Anna stepped across towards Morozov, the weapon trained on him. But Kirsten's eyes were drawn to the girl. She walked away too confidently, calmly.

This sort of thing couldn't happen that often. The girl tiptoed across the floor, not making a sound, not drawing any attention to herself. There was no sign of panic, no sign of tears. She reached down towards her clothing, but she reached towards her jacket first.

The girl was quick. She had grabbed the gun from her jacket, turned, and was ready to fire at Kirsten when Kirsten's bullet hit her. It was a clean shot, followed by a second, which caused Anna Hunt to look over. 'I think this is someone from inside his Service,' said Kirsten.

Anna turned around to Morozov, and demanded, as far as Kirsten could make out, who the girl was.

After he responded, she turned to Kirsten. 'A low-level operative on the way up. A very good assassin, apparently.'

'Not very good at hiding her intentions, though,' said Kirsten. 'She could do with an acting lesson, or she could if she was still here.'

Morozov was now down on his knees. He wasn't crying, but his face was white. Anna Hunt had a reputation wherever she was, and it wasn't born from a woman who played easy. She peppered Morozov with questions in Russian, hitting him with the back of her gun, and Kirsten watched his bloodied face. Several times she hit him.

But he told a story, not that Kirsten could understand any of it. Instead, she watched the bedroom door and listened from afar. The tone of his voice was pleading. He was a man who knew he'd have to talk his way out of this one, have to trust that he could give enough. Clearly, he wasn't expecting any rescue. He had sent his people out, desperate to capture Anna Hunt again, desperate for the woman that would be such a trophy to take to Moscow. But they had turned it around on him. It'd been Kirsten's idea.

'We've been here a while,' said Kirsten. 'We probably should get going. His people will be returning. Have you got what you need from him?

'Yes,' said Anna. 'A lot.'

'Then why are we here?'

Kirsten went to open the door, but Anna hadn't moved. Morozov was on his knees, looking up at Anna Hunt. Anna was standing in front of him. A gun was at her side. Anna was a woman of action as far as Kirsten always knew it. Anna didn't stand before people wondering. She was constantly giving a figure of being in control, but as Kirsten looked at her, she could see her shake, but not from fear. This was anger.

'We need to go,' said Kirsten.

'Soon,' said Anna. 'Soon.'

She said something in Russian and Kirsten saw Morozov's face take on another level of white she hadn't seen. His eyes said he was petrified, terrified, and yet Anna was just standing there, arms by her side. She suddenly picked up a gun, examined it, and checked the silencer. Kirsten walked over and grabbed Anna's arm.

'Come on, we need to go.'

But Anna pushed her away gently. 'Soon,' she said.

Then she straightened up. Her arm went out straight, gun pointed at Morozov's head and she fired two quick shots.

'What the hell,' said Kirsten. 'He gave us what we needed. We didn't need to . . .'

'We did.'

'You think he'd still come after us? You think he would tell people what he told you? He'd be giving himself up. The FSB wouldn't like that. He'd be keeping his head down trying to not let on.'

'He did something to me in their headquarters,' said Anna. She was staring down at the body, shaking, and Kirsten became worried.

'He did what?'

'That nightmare,' she said, 'the nightmare you had, the one I saved you from. He was my nightmare. He said he wanted to own the great Anna Hunt.'

Kirsten saw a tear run down Anna's face. She was shaking, and then she sniffed it back.

'Come on,' she said. 'You're right, of course. We need to go.'

Kirsten stepped forward and spat on the body of Morozov. 'Yes, we do,' she said.

She touched Anna on the shoulder. The woman seemed to almost wake up, like she'd been dozing, drowsy somewhere, and suddenly, an alarm bell had gone off. She wiped a tear off her face. Suddenly, she was Anna Hunt again. She was the great secret agent. Kirsten watched her stride across the room, turn around, and wave Kirsten over.

'It's time to get out of here.'

'Did you get what you needed from him? Did he tell you?'

'He told me plenty.'

'Like what?'

'Later,' said Anna. 'I'll tell you later,' and disappeared out into the corridor.

Chapter 14

The road ahead of them was clear, and it wouldn't be long until they would reach the Finnish border. They wouldn't pass through the Russian checkpoint. Instead, they'd have to stop somewhere short and help Justin get over by an unofficial crossing. Once in Finland, Anna had allies, people she could call upon. They could get a boat back to England and then up to Scotland. They may even fly.

The team were in a blue car and they kept their speed low so as not to attract attention. In truth, they seemed to be so far away from anyone that there was no attention to garner, and Kirsten was breathing easily as she drove along the roads. Beside her, Anna Hunt was deep in contemplation.

Justin was in the rear seat. His foot was still up in the air as best he could put it. He could hobble on it, but he wanted it well-rested before he had to travel across rough ground. His wound had failed to go septic though they checked it a few times, but the bandages in place were not for removing, not till he got to Finland. Once there, he could get better medical help.

The day turned from a cold but bright one into the dark night, the headlights sweeping the road ahead. Kirsten looked at her phone that showed there would be a turnoff soon, a track to go down. They'd follow the track until it got parallel with the border about a mile out. From there, they would have a two-mile walk to find the road on the other side. Once over the border, Anna Hunt would call someone from her past who would help them.

Kirsten appreciated that most of this couldn't have been done without Anna. She'd been in the Service so long, had travelled to so many places—especially Russia—that contacts were available. Kirsten always had to make them. She hadn't been back to where she'd been before. In fact, she hadn't been abroad that many times, either working for or within the Service.

'Is now a good time to talk about what Morozov said?' asked Kirsten.

Anna glared over. 'Yes,' she said, 'of course. Sorry, I've been a little . . .' Kirsten put her hand across, touching Anna's.

'Is there something I don't know about?' asked Justin. 'You've all been quiet, very.'

'When they held me at the headquarters,' said Anna, 'they . . .'

A tear ran down her face, followed by another, and she looked across at Kirsten. Kirsten was trying to drive, not miss her turn, and also felt so deeply for Anna she wanted to hug her. She turned the car off the road and stopped.

'Dear God,' said Justin, 'I'm sorry.'

Anna gave him a nod. 'But he won't do that to anyone else,' she said. 'He won't do that.'

'We'll get you help,' said Kirsten. 'We'll sort that out once we're done, once all of this is sorted.'

Justin was quiet, waiting for the moment between the two

women to subside, but as the silence went on, he spoke up.

'I don't mean to be indelicate,' he said, 'but if we can't get the help sorted until after we're done, can you tell us what Morozov said so we can get done?'

'Of course,' said Anna, giving a sniff. At that moment, Kirsten thought she looked like someone approaching her fifties or even possibly into it. The usual youthful expression wasn't there. Instead, the pain of life was clear on her face.

'Gethsemane is a name for a turned-British operative. She was originally called Lorraine Hurst. Apparently, she was sent to be deep undercover in Russia and operated successfully for a while until Godfrey came over. The two of them became intimate, and she was quite the operative.

'They did a lot of damage, but they raised their profile too much and ended up becoming trapped on a train. As Morozov told it, the KGB was coming along the train, searching it. Godfrey had popped out of the carriage and had seen them. He didn't, however, warn her. Instead, he moved deeper into the train, left her to be caught and taken off the train. At which point, with everyone distracted, he was gone. As a spy, she was taken away, tortured—unimaginable things, no doubt. She wasn't that old. Just a kid and then the worst of it comes.'

'What?' asked Justin.

'Nobody did anything to get her. Nobody tried to intervene, not even in diplomatic channels. Godfrey didn't even acknowledge she was gone. Few knew about her; nature of the Service and that. She was truly abandoned by Godfrey. Apparently, they'd talked of marriage, of setting up somewhere, of children.'

'Really?' said Justin. 'I find that difficult to believe.'

'Morozov told me, and there's really no reason to lie about

that. What haunts me is the fact that when he came back from Russia, that's when we first met. I was in his bed within three months of that,' said Anna.

Kirsten was shocked. Anna didn't divulge information easily, especially about Godfrey and her. Clearly, there'd been more to their professional relationship than good colleagues.

'What haunts me,' said Anna, 'is when I got caught in Russia, he didn't come for me either, but I got back out. I understand where that's all coming from. I feel I understand Gethsemane. Morozov said she turned. She was their operative, their spy. He said that she was hunting Godfrey for revenge, not to take down the Service out of revenge. She wouldn't do that. It's not about the Service. The Service didn't fail her, Godfrey did.'

'But Godfrey is the Service. Is he not?' asked Kirsten.

'No, he's not. He might be the head of the Service, but he is not the Service. The Service is something else,' said Anna. 'Don't forget it. The Service is a layer of protection for our country, and many good people have given their lives for it. It's a dark place. A place that you need to be clever to operate in. A place of awkward morals, hard decisions, betrayal, deceit, the lot. But it's a necessary evil . . . and at times, it's a very righteous instrument.'

Kirsten wasn't so sure that she agreed with Anna on this, but she kept quiet, letting the woman speak.

'Morozov,' said Anna, 'was a good KSB agent. He probably knew his time had come. After what he'd done to me, he would have known his time was coming. And his last statement was about revenge. She was coming for revenge, but I don't think so. If she's an agent, she won't come in unless they've told her to. And they wouldn't sanction simple revenge. That's not how they work, especially against such a target. She'd have no backup. She'd have no use of the contacts over there if she did it on the quiet. They'd find out and they would take her out. She's a loose cannon. She's doing this because she's been instructed to.'

'So, what are they seeking?' asked Justin. 'Just to undermine the Service? Just to . . .'

'No,' said Anna, 'keep driving, Kirsten.' Kirsten started the car up again, got back on the road and continued to drive.

'Listen,' said Anna, 'there comes a time when you have to trust people, and I'm trusting you with this, both of you. Godfrey has a place of secrets. He truly doesn't have faith in the electrical systems. He fears the ability to hack into systems of an electrical nature.'

'A wise man,' said Justin.

'Indeed,' said Anna, 'but he has all this information. At some point, he would know that if he died, the information would have to be passed on. There is a place for items to be passed on to the new head of the Service. Most people think you would just hand over access to the files on the computers. Not Godfrey. The real information, especially about very deep and very secret agents, is not held in the systems.

'These are the people working at the heart of governments, royal families, deep inside terrorist organisations to the level of almost being a leader. They're operating on a level where the lines are blurred, and we don't need to have public scrutiny over what they've done. It would mean you could never run a contact like that again. But all the information has to be somewhere. Godfrey has that somewhere.'

'Where is it?' asked Kirsten.

'I don't know,' said Anna, 'I truly don't. If I did, I would go there and secure it because that's what they're looking for.'

'How do you know it exists?' asked Justin. 'Godfrey wouldn't share a secret like that.'

'No, he wouldn't,' said Anna. She shuffled in her seat. 'Let me tell you a story about Godfrey. He does like his women and he likes them from the Service. He likes a woman who can handle herself the way he can. But he also has a distance between us. He will hand her over, he will happily let her do whatever, or have whatever happen to her, to further his cause within the Service.

'In that sense, he's a dispassionate lover. He abandoned me in Russia, and I got out. We had words. But more than that, I was worried that he had another woman. I didn't understand him fully. I didn't understand the way he was, that he couldn't form a proper emotional relationship. All he could do was use you, to a point. He wasn't nasty about it. He wasn't deliberately mean, it's just the way he is. The man's soulless at the depths of it.

'But he is a heck of an operator. So, I set about trying to find out as much as I could about him and I knew he went somewhere. Somewhere his own staff didn't know. Brenda didn't know. And when he came back from this place, he would come back with information and pass out certain instructions. He also went there when he had a lot of detail on his mind.

'That was him making his notes. That was him filing and controlling his system. There is a place, wherever it is, that Godfrey has and it's Godfrey's secret. It's his mind. And it's all on paper so he can beat the computers and the hackers. He's never been good at that and had to leave that to someone else. Godfrey doesn't have faith in things he has to leave for someone else. He always protects it. If that information gets out, the Service as we know it won't just be falling apart; there

117

will be bloodshed across the world. No countries will trust our country because we are everywhere. Even with our allies, we spy on them. As everyone does. That place of Godfrey's cannot be allowed to fall. He will be nowhere near it,' said Anna. 'That's the one good thing at the moment.'

Kirsten turned the car off down the track, following it round and then stopping. She stared at her phone.

'I think this is it,' she said. 'I think we're nearly somewhere safe.'

'Safe?' said Justin. 'There's nowhere safe at the moment. We might go out of the spider's lair, but back home is a rat's nest. We should be very careful about how we go back in.'

'The people I have here in Finland will be fine. They're outside of any Service. Ours, Finnish, or any other country. I know some genuinely decent people in this world,' said Anna. 'Now, wrap up. Let's get you over there, Justin.'

Together, the three walked a mile to the border. There was a wire and a fence of sorts, and there was supposed to be a guard that came past every so often. But out here, it was easy. They got Justin up and over, joined him, and they walked a mile into Finland.

They came close to a road and Anna Hunt made a call. As they shivered, a minibus pulled up, which they climbed into. In the front seat were a man and a woman, both in their late sixties, Kirsten would have said. The man had a rough, greying beard. The woman's hair had thinned and lost its lustre. She smiled with a toothy grin; he didn't seem to smile at all.

Kirsten sat back as the minibus pulled away, taking them to safety somewhere. The game was truly afoot, she thought. They'd come all this way, got into Russia, stirred up a right palaver, come out the other side, and yet, they were going to walk into worse. The stakes were high, but mixed in with that was Craig.

Beside Kirsten, Anna Hunt was struggling. She put her arm around Anna, pulled her close, and Anna laid her head across Kirsten's chest. Tears flowed. Kirsten looked down at the woman. She was hard; she was tough as nails, and yet, what they'd done to her. Kirsten leaned down and kissed Anna's head, then ran her fingers through her hair. It always took a toll, this place, this Service they were in. She wasn't coming back, she told herself. Once this was sorted, she was never coming back.

Chapter 15

I t was four days later when the trio arrived back in Scotland. Initially, they'd come in via Harwich in the southeast of England, taken a car and driven up. On route, they had a discussion of the best way to go about dealing with the current situation of the Service, and of finding Gethsemane.

'The way I see it,' said Anna, 'we've got two options here. We know Craig and Mark Lamb have been involved with Gethsemane. So, we could hunt them down, come in from that angle, drive the Scottish connection. Or we find Godfrey. It won't be easy, but they're hunting for Godfrey. Godfrey's got the golden ticket. If they get him and they get to his stash of secrets, that's the country screwed over. That'll be bedlam in terms of the international community. At worst, we need to torch that place, assuming we can even find it.'

'How do you find Godfrey?' asked Kirsten.

She was behind the wheel of a hired Vauxhall Astra with classical musical on the radio. This was because it was Justin's choice for the next two hours. They'd already endured Anna Hunt's heavy metal, something which shocked Kirsten to the core. Anna had explained working in Finland and in Russia for such a long time gave her an appreciation for the genre. A lot of the characters she'd taken on would have had this sort of music as their staple. Anna had become immersed in it and ultimately liked it. It wasn't for Kirsten.

'How do you find Godfrey?' asked Kirsten. 'He's a true operator. You said that yourself, Anna. How do you bring him to task? The only time I've ever been with him, he's come to me and found me, or he's been on Service property. He will not be on Service property anymore. He's actively keeping out of the way. If he hadn't been aware people were coming for him, then maybe, I could see, just maybe, we might do it. I don't see how we do it when he knows they're coming.'

'She'll find him,' said Anna. 'She will find him. He's good. He's very good, but nobody is perfect. The other thing about Godfrey is he has changed little. She'll understand him. She was with him longer than me. Certainly, in an intimate sense, so if anybody really knows Godfrey, it will be Gethsemane.'

'Craig and Mark Lamb are somewhere we've gone before,' said Kirsten. 'They'll see us coming as well. Craig is an operator. Craig knows that I'm not on his side. He'll be difficult.'

'But not impossible. The problem from that side is,' Anna said, 'that Gethsemane is still there. You can get with Craig and get with Mark Lamb, but you've still got to go through Gethsemane then, after that. She's a problem if she sees it happening. We're on the rough side of this. They're dictating the narrative. They forced Godfrey onto the run.'

'I hate to say it,' said Justin from the back, 'but you ladies are correct, and personally, I think both are bad ideas.'

'What do you mean?' asked Anna.

Justin pulled himself up in the rear seat of the car. His foot was better than it had been, but he was still hobbling when not being driven.

'The way I look at it,' said Justin, 'is that maybe we need to find Godfrey, not to win him over, but to bring him into the sights of Gethsemane. We need to draw her out, and then we can ambush them. This will not be an ending with Gethsemane heading home, fed up she couldn't get anywhere. We've gone too far. She's already turned the Service upside down from underneath. The only reason it hasn't been completed so far is Godfrey . . . Godfrey being good.

'There could be a protracted search. That won't help us. The Service will be out of action. Things will be a mess. Other issues the Service deals with, other countries, things will spiral out of control. But if we can find Godfrey, and if we can bring him into the light so they can see him, but they don't think it's us that's done it, they may just come after him. More than that, if we get to him first, he may even go with the plan. He may put himself out there like bait on a hook.'

'He'll have to be forced into that,' said Anna. 'Truly. Godfrey looks after himself. He has that sharp demeanour that makes him look business-like, but underneath it, Godfrey protects himself. All excellent operators should. We should have an eye on ourselves. The ones that don't end up dead quickly.'

'True,' said Justin, 'so maybe he doesn't need to know. But this will end with a bullet in someone's head. Too many major players. Too many major players to go away. You're not going away,' he said to Anna. She stared back at him for a moment, grim-faced.

'And thank God for that. Kirsten and I, we can fade away, but you're Service to the core. You're the country to the core,' said Justin. 'Godfrey is Service to the core. His baby—it's become something he owns. He won't want to see it go down, and Gethsemane has come too far. She isn't going back to Russia after she's turned the tables like this. No, this will end with somebody getting a bullet in their head. Somebody will come out on top as a victor and it has to be you, Anna. It must be you.'

Kirsten pulled over into the services as the conversation in the car died. Bizet was playing in the background and it was light. Kirsten wished they had the heavy metal back on because at least that drowned out every other thought she had, even if she didn't appreciate it.

The three stopped at an eatery on the motorway, sitting down to chips and chicken nuggets. They'd rather have something a bit more appetising, but they were in a rush, and it was there. Justin was just thankful there was a seat.

The motorway services were busy. People rushing here and there, and the three were lost in the crowd. They were sure they hadn't been spotted driving up from the south. Craig and Mark Lamb were still based up in Scotland, as far as they were aware. Godfrey had been up in Scotland. The nature of Scotland as opposed to England was that it had a small number of population for the size of the country.

There were wild areas, away from everyone. It wasn't quite Canada, but it had places you could disappear to, places you could be out of reach easily. Anna thought that Godfrey's stack of secrets was somewhere within Scotland. Where, she didn't know; she based it on the time it took for him to come back from there, his visits. It was an assumption, but it wasn't a crass one.

Justin stood up and said he was going for a walk to stretch his leg. It was clearly sore, and the women watched him hobble off. Kirsten looked down at her coffee. It was inside a paper cup with a plastic lid and she'd barely touched it.

'It is pretty rubbish, isn't it?' said Anna, almost laughing.

'Are you okay?' asked Kirsten.

'No,' said Anna. 'Do not even think I am okay. Inside on that side of things, I am a mess. I dreamt last night of it happening again. I will need help.'

'And we'll get you it. I'll be here for you. You've always seen something in me, Anna. You've always been there. We work well together, you and I.'

'I thought once you might be someone to come in and take over the Service one day, years in the future, mind.'

'What about you? You should lead it.'

Anna stared back at Kirsten, her eyes heavy. 'Why should I lead it?'

'Because you're tough. You've seen many places in the world. You know how things operate.'

'I have, and I'll defend my country to the hilt. But no, I don't want to be head of the Service. I'm like you. I want to be out in the field. Love the excitement, the danger. And I don't kill people lightly. I know you don't; you justify what you do. You have to. Let me tell you that remaining firm on that justification is difficult, the older you get.

'I've had to stand by and watch Godfrey as he's done things. I've had to stand by and rationalise that all of this action from the Service was justified in defending our country. Our country is safe because of what we did. Some of it's so unpalatable. These days I don't know, Kirsten. These days I do not know. Look at me now. I've been in this Service thirty-four years.'

'What age were you when you started?' asked Kirsten.

'Seventeen,' said Anna. 'I know, I shouldn't have been there, but I was. I started working in the office as a secretary, but I was curious. They caught me two years later, knowing secrets way above my station. I thought I was going to get put in prison, but Godfrey promoted me. He saw the potential. I thought he saw someone he could love as well. A dumb little girl I was then. I didn't understand how these things worked. I certainly didn't understand him. Maybe I was lucky when it all fell apart between us. You weren't. Craig and you were good. Circumstance blew him apart. Circumstance.'

'What we had wasn't strong enough,' said Kirsten. 'I'm realising that now. I guess I had rose-tinted glasses as well.'

'You know you have to work at it. You know it just doesn't come like that,' said Anna.

'If you don't want to do the Service, head it when this is all done, what do you want to do?' asked Kirsten suddenly. 'I understand you're here working for your country. You want to put things right, but when it's all put right, you go back into the Service. Do you become lackey to someone else?'

'Lackey? When have I ever been a lackey?'

'I suppose not,' said Kirsten. 'But what do you want to do?'

'Honestly, I want to go to South America. I want to swim in the ocean down there. Find somebody that wants to spend the next thirty, forty years of their life with me and die old with me. I want somebody who doesn't need to be running across the worst areas of the world getting themselves into scrapes to excite me. I want somebody whose company I can sit in and be at peace and be happy with.

'All this danger, Kirsten, all this excitement, all this fuel. It's because I'm not happy. I need something. Do you know that Godfrey's the only love I've ever had in my life? And he was a bad one. And I've never really pushed him away because of my love for the country. I think I'm owed my time now.'

'Do you think you'll ever find someone who could love you after what you've done?' asked Kirsten.

'I don't know if I'll find someone I could tell the truth to—tell all the truth to—who could love me.'

'Who knows?' said Kirsten. 'But I tell you what, South America sounds good. The beach, the sea, sounds good to me.'

Kirsten stood up and looked around for Justin. She saw the man hobbling, almost excited, and he was pointing.

'What's he pointing at?' asked Kirsten.

'He'll be finding coffee. He didn't take coffee with his chicken nuggets and chips meal. I think he's been stung like that before.'

'Where do we go then? Where do we go to plan this?'

'We go up north,' said Anna. 'We go to Dores just outside Inverness.'

'Dores? You used to meet Macleod and others there. It's your favourite haunt, Loch Ness, for meeting the police service.'

'I have a place there,' said Anna. 'My place, not a safe house. My place is there. Sometimes you need the water,' she said. 'You need to watch the ripples. You need to let the mind dissolve the troubles into that water. And yes, it's also a pleasant spot to meet the local police.' She smiled. 'Justin's found coffee. What are we doing here? Let's get some, then we're off to Dores.'

As she went to walk, Kirsten grabbed her by the arm. 'Justin isn't fit enough for this fight,' she said. 'With that leg, he's not quick enough. He can't be in the field with the likes of Craig or Gethsemane about. He'll die.'

'And that's also why we're going to Dores. Some people in

Dores complain about Wi-Fi speeds, access to the international hub being non-existent. I think Justin will find that my house is better equipped.'

'Whatever comes,' said Kirsten to Anna, 'I don't regret meeting you.'

'Neither do I,' said Anna. 'You remind me of me. Just a better version.'

'Coffee?' said Kirsten.

'Coffee,' said Anna. 'Anything better than the muck back there.'

Chapter 16

Anna Hunt stood on the shores of Loch Ness, staring out at the water. Kirsten could see her as she crossed the road down onto the small beach. Over the previous days, sometimes Anna would just go quiet. Kirsten had never seen her like this. Anna was always professional, on the go, busy. Now she faced one of the biggest fights of their lives in terms of the Service, and yet she would go distant.

The trauma of what happened to Anna in Russia was clearly eating away at her. Constantly gnawing at her. Kirsten had wanted out of the Service and she'd gone with Craig, happy in the knowledge of leaving it behind, but she didn't hate it. Anna had been there for over thirty years, and yet now, she seemed to be almost distant from it, regretful to a point.

Kirsten walked up behind her and put her hands on Anna's shoulders, rubbing them.

'The thoughts coming back again?'

'Did I wake you during the night? I thought you'd be okay in other rooms, but . . .'

'I heard you scream,' said Kirsten. 'I've never heard you scream, but I heard you and it scared me.'

'It scared me, too,' said Anna.

She didn't turn to look at Kirsten, but kept looking out at the water. Kirsten dropped her arms and wrapped them around Anna's waist, pulling her in tight.

'You'll get there; you'll get there.'

'Have you ever had a sister?' asked Anna. 'No, you didn't, did you? You had a brother. Your brother needed help.'

'He did, and he was different, but my brother could also hug me. He was bigger,' said Kirsten. 'Sometimes when I was younger and I felt bad, or I was down, he couldn't communicate because of the way he was. All he could do was empathise. He did that by wrapping his arms around me. It didn't solve the problem. He couldn't make it go away, but what he did meant so much to me.' Kirsten squeezed tighter.

'I've never had any brothers or sisters,' said Anna. 'I was always on my own. I grew up through Barnardo's as a child, an orphan. Never knew my parents. When you work in this job, the one thing you certainly don't get is a hug.' Anna moved her arms down, placing her hands on Kirsten's. 'Thank you.' she said. 'Your analogy's right. You can't make it go away. You can't fight it for me, but it is better having you here.'

Kirsten smiled, but her mind was also on other matters. 'Where would Godfrey go? Where would Godfrey's stash be?'

'I've been thinking about that,' said Anna. 'I believe we need to visit his driver.'

'His driver? Craig was his driver for a while. Didn't think Godfrey had a specific driver.'

'He had many drivers. It's part of the Service plan so they don't know where you are. They're not all privy to it. There's a certain secrecy around it, but Godfrey had his favourite driver.'

'Who is . . .?'

'George,' said Anna. 'George is a Yorkshireman, quite gruff,

129

speaks his mind, but a proper chauffeur. Knows his place when opening doors. Handy enough with a gun, but wasn't the best in that respect. In saying that, Godfrey could look after himself, so he didn't need someone running point. If he did, he had Brenda, but George retired about three years ago. Whenever Godfrey was on a job that no one knew about, George was taking him there.'

'With all due respect,' asked Kirsten, 'how do you know that? If it's a job that nobody knows about, how did you know?'

'Godfrey would disappear. He's the head of the Service. He didn't have to say where he was going, but often he did. If it interlinked with what different departments were doing, what different sections were doing, then he would just go. If he took David or Jane, usually you found out about it afterwards. It was something maybe mundane, possibly a meeting with her Majesty back then, something of that ilk, but with George, you never found out where he had been. Never. Those were always with George. George is the key here. George will know where he's been.'

'What sort of man is George?' asked Kirsten. 'If he's a diehard, if he's faithful, you'll not get a word out of him.'

'George is practical,' said Anna.

'So what? We just meet George? Go ask him?'

'No, it won't be that easy. George will be a target for a start. He'll be very wary about others. He might've been retired for three years, but he'll know what's going on. Nobody ever leaves the Service after all,' said Anna, smiling at Kirsten. 'When you left, you still maintained the old guards, still kept yourself aware of what was happening. George will be exactly the same.

'As I recall,' she continued, 'he had a flat in London. He was a Yorkshireman, but he had family down that way. I also think he liked the cricket when it was down in London. I remember that about him, being in the car with Godfrey and the cricket was on. Well, Godfrey never liked cricket. That was another thing.' said Anna. 'Godfrey let him put on the radio what he wanted to put on. Godfrey never let the other ones put on anything like that. Wasn't their choice. Godfrey would put on what he wanted. George was a special driver.'

'What about Justin?'

'I'm assuming he can cook for himself,' said Anna.

'He's not going down with us?'

'No.' said Anna. 'We'll take the sleeper train down and we'll take it back up. Leave Justin up here, but he can also start running more intelligence gathering. Go looking for contacts that way. It's what he does best, anyway.'

'Okay.' said Kirsten. She gave Anna another hug, and then the women turned and walked back to the house. The house wasn't large, but it had an underground section. Somebody back in the eighties had feared that there would be a nuclear strike and had built themselves an underground shelter. When Anna had bought the property, she had done so because of that shelter.

Down below was a myriad of computer banks, a base away from everything. A place that was personal to her. Justin hadn't known about it despite having worked with her for all those years, and now he was getting access. It enthralled him, but it said something else to Kirsten. Anna was slowly signing out. If your base was compromised, your private section, that was because you didn't need it anymore. If Anna thought she did, she would have kept it a secret. She would never have let on about it, taking them to some other safe house.

Justin was happy in his role, saying that his foot needed rest. But he booked them on the sleeper train that night. The two travelled lightly, armed with only a handgun and a rucksack each.

During the trip down, Kirsten took the top bunk of the sleeper train. The cabin, small but with enough room to stand and to dress in, wasn't soundproof from those next door. The pair spoke nothing of what they were going to do, but discussed such things as Kirsten's family.

She talked a lot about her brother, in whom Anna was deeply interested. Anna, in turn, told Kirsten about growing up as a Barnardo's child and made the joke that she was never in any of the adverts for Barnardo's because they didn't see the Service as being a great advert. They didn't want them to think that they were groomed into being a spy. Of course, no one from her past knew Anna was a spy, but Kirsten had liked to joke.

They stepped out around eight in the morning into London, leaving from the nearby Euston Station to catch the Underground across the city. George's flat was twelve floors up and had a glass front George could see out of. Kirsten and Anna looked up at the towering building in front of them. George's flat was up there, but Kirsten thought something was wrong. She pulled a small pair of binoculars out of her backpack and looked off into the distance somewhere, hopefully gauging the right height. She then turned, swinging the binoculars slowly. As she scanned past the building, she realised that George's flat was extremely blackened.

She walked over to the door at the foot of the flats. 'Excuse me,' said Kirsten to a doorman, 'one of my friends has a flat here. He said there was a bit of trouble. Might have been a fire.'

'That's correct, ma'am,' said the doorman. 'About three days ago, we had a fire up there. There's been a bit of moving back and forth since. About three of the flats are burnt out or near enough. They all got out, though. Everyone was okay. Still not sure how it started. It'll probably be one of these electrical things. Dishwasher. Tumble dryer. You know the sort.'

'Where did all the residents go?' asked Kirsten.

'You don't have anyone living here, do you?' said the man suddenly.

'No,' said Kirsten. 'Sorry.'

'Local paper, is it?'

Kirsten nodded.

'You're just doing your job, but I can't talk about them. They're all safe, but I can't talk about where they went. You'll have to hunt them down on your own if you want that story.'

'Fair enough,' said Kirsten. She made her way back over to Anna. 'George has moved out of the flat. Went on fire with three others. Sounds to me like someone's been hunting him.'

'He'll be watching for them,' said Anna. 'Why don't you watch his flat very conspicuously? Make sure you're out in front. I'll take a quieter line,' said Anna.

Kirsten nodded and made her way over to a coffee shop just across from the towering block. The thing about having flats in an area like this was there were plenty of food stores, barber shops, everything you needed for daily life close by. Whereas a village would have them laid out in the middle with the houses surrounding, here the flats went up. At the bottom, on street level, were all the amenities and services you required.

It was a gorgeous day in London. Kirsten could sit outside, proudly watching the burned flats up above. It took three coffees and a desire for some dinner before anything happened. She'd finished a coffee, looked over and saw a small food outlet doing rice, chicken and other things in a box and thought she would sit in there. Again, she'd be close to the flats.

As she walked over, she suddenly felt someone grab her shoulder. Kirsten could have easily shrugged off the attack and incapacitated her attacker. It was a man in a long trench coat with a wide-brimmed hat, but she let him push her into an alleyway. She also let him push her against a wall, place a gun into her chest and then frisk her down either side.

He reached into her backpack behind her, took the gun out from it, and put it in his pocket. He then turned her around and frisked down the back. As she faced the wall, he said to her, 'Three coffees. Three coffees you had watching that building. Why? Who are you looking for?'

'I'm looking for no one,' said Kirsten. The man spoke in a thick Yorkshire accent, so Kirsten reckoned she knew who it was. But George and she had never met. Never seen each other in all their travels.

'There's a problem at the moment. People not being where they should be. I have a feeling this has been too easy. Tell me, love, if you're from the newspaper. Because if you are, you've stumbled into a world that you don't want to be in. You need to own up to me now.'

He turned her round and reached inside her jacket for some ID. There was a wallet, but it only had credit cards in it. He read the name. 'Did they turn you too?'

The man suddenly wasn't pressing the gun as hard into Kirsten's front. He'd gone silent. Kirsten saw a gun pointed at the man's head.

'Let's all just calm down a bit.' It was Anna's voice. 'Hello,

George. It's been a while. We need to chat. I told Kirsten you were a good operative, you were an excellent driver, and you had Godfrey's trust. Of course, what I forgot to mention was you were pretty rubbish with the field craft. Second person, George. Always be looking for the second person, especially when somebody is so obvious.'

'Miss Hunt, I take it they haven't turned you.' The man handed Kirsten's gun back into her open hand.

'We'll have to find out, George,' said Anna. 'We'll have to find out just where you stand first, George.'

Chapter 17

'Where are you living, George?' asked Anna, her gun still on the man. 'I'd rather not discuss things on the street. That way we can make this a lot more civilised.'

'It's me, though, isn't it,' said George. 'We can put the gun down. We can walk and talk normally like civilised people.'

'No, George, we can't. We need to go somewhere we can defend from. If we're out in the café, there are too many cars going past. I need to focus on what you're saying and not be constantly watching all around me. Where are you living at the moment?'

'I'll take you there,' he said.

'No,' said Anna, 'you're not listening. Where do you live?'

'Around the block. There was a flat free, so I took it. Under a different name, of course.'

'Of course,' said Anna. 'From there, you can watch easily who's coming and going, and who's coming towards your old flat. Why are you doing that, though?'

'I thought you wanted off the street,' said George. 'I'll tell you inside.'

'Lead on,' said Anna, and she put her arm around George as

136

they walked, her gun back inside its holster. 'What I will say is you mess me about, I'll break your neck.'

'I know the score,' said the man.

Kirsten followed behind the pair and realised how stocky George was. He wasn't tall, but he was square with thick-set legs. He could probably handle himself to a degree in a fight, but he was a driver. His skill set would have been slightly different. No doubt he could handle a car, and he probably could shoot a weapon reasonably well, but he wasn't the trained operatives that Anna and Kirsten were. Their role was out in the field; their role was taking people down. George's was much more about protection.

George did indeed now live around the corner, and after walking around, he entered a complex of flats less than five hundred metres away from his old one. They went up three flights of stairs, and then George took out a key and opened up into a bedsit.

In the far corner was the bed. There was a sofa and a chair in the middle with a TV sitting opposite. Along the back wall was a small kitchenette, and the toilet and bathroom were off to one side.

'Hope your last place was a bit more interesting than this,' said Anna, looking around the room.

'This is temporary.'

'Well, I wish you well, George,' said Anna, 'but I need to know why were you watching? Why were you watching your flat? Were you hoping they would come back after burning it?'

'No,' he said. 'I burnt it, I burnt it down to the ground. Or at least to the bottom of my floor.'

'Why?' asked Kirsten.

George had taken up a position on the main sofa, and Anna

had sat down in the single seat near him. Kirsten stood up, leaning against the wall. She wouldn't sit down in case she had to hasten. There was only one way into this bedsit, and there would be one way out. She couldn't risk being sloppy in case anybody followed them.

'Somebody came to see me,' said George. 'I don't know who they are, but I had a rather unpleasant conversation.'

'Tell me about it,' said Anna.

'I'm sitting in the pub. It's the Clown's Red Nose around the corner. Just sitting doing my crossword—had a pint of bitter beside me—and in comes this blonde. I mean, that pub, it's not that sort of pub. You don't get young blondes coming into it, certainly not dressed the way she was. One leg half sticking out from a dress that clung to her. There are only about three other guys in the pub, because it's eleven in the morning, but she wanders over and asks me what I'm drinking. I said I'm fine, but she didn't go to anybody else. Instead, she sits down beside me. It wasn't very subtle. I told her I'd rather be left alone because I'd got my crossword to do, but she asked me had I seen Godfrey lately?

'Of course, I said no. I said to her I was retired. She replied that there was some turmoil within the Service.'

'How much do you know about the turmoil in the Service?' asked Anna.

'I know all about the turmoil in the Service. Retired, yes, but I'm not dead. I didn't let her know that. Just said I didn't work for them anymore. Anyway, she produces several notes and places them beside me. She's also got that bare leg sitting beside me; takes my hand and puts it on her thigh. Says that there's more money, and there are opportunities for other things if I come and have a chat with them. I said, "Why, what use was I?"'

'I take it she knew exactly who you were,' asked Anna.

'She said I was his driver, said that I might know certain locations. I told her I was out. She gave me this cock and bull story about the Service having changed, Godfrey being the enemy. I said I'd signed the Official Secrets Act. I couldn't be telling things like that. The Service would have to bring me back in, ask me officially. Even then, it'd be difficult to betray a confidence.'

'Good,' said Anna, 'but . . .?'

'Well, she said to me she would call around later that evening to see if I could give her a better answer. She took the money, and she took herself outside.'

'Were you tempted?' asked Kirsten.

George looked up at her, a rather quizzical look on his face. 'I don't know. The money, I've got enough. I'm sitting in a pub doing a crossword drinking bitter at eleven o'clock in the morning. I mean, how much better does life get? Her? That's that funny thing, isn't it?

'Part of me is looking and thinking, o*h, yes.* Another part of me is thinking, *she's too good to be true. She's probably going to be boring* because that would be my luck, wouldn't it? It's like women when they get me; they think there's some sort of razzle-dazzle, rapid repartee, because with a face this ugly, he must have something.'

The comment made Kirsten smile, but Anna remained serious throughout.

'Tell me, George, what did you do next?'

'Well, I knew what was happening within the Service, and if they came back, it wouldn't be pretty. So, I set fire to my flat. I sat, and I watched. She came back that night, three of them with her. They stayed downstairs. She went up. Then she realised the flat was burnt. But she was going up to bed me. She was going up to get an answer out of me one way or another. If that didn't work, the heavy mob was coming in. I clocked them all, though. I was quite happy with myself. Managed to avoid everyone until you two.'

'You know what they were looking for, don't you?' asked Anna.

'You tell me,' said George.

'Godfrey's stash. He never told you where it was. But if you were his driver, his favourite driver, you were the one that he trusted, and you probably dropped him close to it. He probably said, "I'm good here, George. You take a walk or give me the car and I'll be back."'

Kirsten noticed that George's eyes were raised slightly at that point. That was the one. He got dropped off by Godfrey.

'I'm not sure what you mean,' said George.

'Yes, you are,' said Kirsten. 'You gave it away. He dropped you off. You maybe had a day or two swanning about. Quite nice, really. A day or two off. Had a phone on you, just in case he needed to come back quickly. The time would've been enough for Godfrey to learn, to build what he was doing, to make his notes.'

'Then to file them in his stash,' said Anna. 'I need you to tell me the places you took him, the places he told you not to tell anyone about. He won't have told you all of them, these secret places, but you would've had to have taken him to the one we want.'

'You're asking me to betray a confidence,' said George. 'I don't see that's right. I don't see . . .'

Anna was on her feet. She had an arm around his throat,

and she picked the man literally up off the couch with his legs wiggling in the air. She turned and drove him up against the wall.

'Frankly, I don't give a toss what you think. I don't give a toss what confidence you had before. You're going to tell me where these places were, or I'll turn you into a vegetable. You're in the way, George. My way. These people, they don't just want to go after Godfrey. They want his secrets. They want to bring down the entire country. Who do you think's after him?'

'It's an ex-lover, isn't it? Basically, it's an ex-lover. Well, they can swing for all the ex-lovers.'

'No, it's not. It's Russia, George. It's Russia. They're going to take all his secrets. There are going to be colleagues dying in countries around the world. We're going to piss off so many other nations because they'll find out we've been spying on them. The enemies. That's bad enough, but they know that already. Our allies, our allies, will have proof. People will get rounded up. People will get tortured.'

'You're still asking me to break a confidence,' said George.

Anna drove a punch into the man's stomach, causing him to wince, but she was holding him there with her right hand on his throat, legs still off the floor. There was a strength in Anna that you never saw from the smart suits on the outside.

'Don't be coy with me, George. Don't mess me about.'

'Can you prove it was Russians?'

Anna Hunt leaned close to George. 'I don't need to prove it was Russians. They did something to me. They did something to me that . . .'

Kirsten thought she was going to lose it. She reached over, and tapped Anna's arm. 'I'll take it,' she said. 'I'll take it from here.' Anna let the man's feet touch the floor before letting go

141

of his throat and she turned away.

'We've just been to Russia,' said Kirsten. 'A woman called Gethsemane is coming, but you probably know that already. How long were you in the Service?'

'Years. I was in years.'

'Always as a driver?' asked Kirsten.

'Yes,' said George.

'You ever do the runs over to Russia?'

'I was the initial courier to get people into Russia,' said George. 'I wasn't always just a lackey for the boss.'

'Did you take over a certain Lorraine Hurst?'

George's face went white. 'Lorraine Hurst? Can't be. She went missing out there.'

'She was left behind by Godfrey, except she wasn't. Lorraine turned traitor. She's coming for him now, but the Russians have sent her over. The Russians want the stash. Godfrey's only good to them for information. If they get a hold of the stash, they've got all the information they could ever want.'

'He never liked that,' said George. He went to walk away from the wall and Kirsten let him. Anna Hunt was now sitting down on the couch. Her eyes were moist with tears. George walked around and sat down beside her.

'Listen,' said Anna, 'I have pursued Gethsemane across to Russia. I found out who she is. It has cost me. Cost one of my people a bullet in the leg. It's cost me something much more valuable, but if the secrets get out, it will cost us everything, including what you worked so hard for, George.'

'He once told me something about you,' said George. 'Anna Hunt,' he said, 'and then he just sighed and then he gave me that look men do when they're thinking about something else. Usually a woman. But he turned to me and he said she's not just an excellent operator, she's actually a good person behind it. But she's able to get rid of the good person every now and again.

'I always thought that was a shame,' he said, 'but I guess being a good person isn't ideal for what we did. If what you're saying is true, there are a couple of places to look. Banbury in Oxfordshire. He had a place out there, I'm sure of it. There was also Glasgow, somewhere on the edge of Glasgow. He used to drop me in Glasgow, but he also went further west, Largs. He collected me in Largs before.'

'On the west coast?' asked Anna. 'It sounds promising. Do you know where he went there?'

'The thing about Godfrey was he was very good, or at least he thought he was. I hear Brenda has turned on him. Well, I never trusted her. He also trusted me too much. I followed him. I followed him because I wanted to know what I didn't know. That's the problem of the Service, isn't it? You want to know everything. Even the things you shouldn't know.

'I was just a driver. I just set down and picked up from wherever, but no, I had to understand Godfrey and where he was going. He holds a rental on a caravan in the caravan park in Largs. It's up near the back of it. I doubt that this time of year it'll be open, the caravan park, but that will not bother Godfrey. If it is his hideout, it'll be minimal.'

'If this is a windup, if you are sending me to somewhere that doesn't have—' started Anna.

'I trust you because Godfrey had a trust in you, or rather, he'd have trusted that you would serve the country. He had more of a trust that you would do it than he would. I knew what he meant. Godfrey was wed to the Service. The Service was his bride. Sorry it didn't work out between the two of you.

143

He mentioned it once.'

Anna stood up, and George followed, extending his hand.

'Good luck to you. I know it's not an extensive list I've given you, but it's the best I can do.'

'I wouldn't wait about here,' said Anna. 'Gethsemane, her people, they're good. They're very good. Quit this flat. Go somewhere else. In fact, get out of London. Get away. We'll try to finish this and end it soon. Until then, get out. A waste of our time if you die now.'

'I guess it is,' he said. 'I guess it truly is.'

Kirsten and Anna turned and walked away down the steps of the flat complex. 'Back north we go,' said Anna.

'Ever been to Largs?' asked Kirsten.

'No,' said Anna.

'Holidayed there with my brother once. It was fun. He liked it. Don't see why it would have attracted Godfrey.'

'That's exactly what he would want you to think,' said Anna. 'Time to go catch our train back north.'

Chapter 18

There wasn't an extensive list of places that Godfrey had snuck off to. Anna and Kirsten were not sure that any of them were where the secret stash was, but they could be where Godfrey was. Largs felt right to Anna, and on the sleeper train back up to Inverness, they decided it would be the place to visit. That night, as they slept in the bunks again, Kirsten became aware that Anna had climbed out of her bed below. She was standing facing the mirror on the door in the cabin, staring at herself. There were quiet tears being cried.

Kirsten switched on the small reading light by the top of her bunk, causing Anna to almost jump.

'Are you okay?' asked Kirsten. Swinging her legs out from underneath the small duvet that covered the bed, she dropped onto the floor of the cabin. She took up Anna's waist in her arms.

'What do you see in there?' said Anna.

'Something special,' said Kirsten. 'Something special.'

'I see something broken.'

'I didn't think it would affect you like this,' said Kirsten. 'I thought you were . . .'

'Stronger? You were going to say stronger. No one's strong enough for this sort of thing. It's deeper. It's more—' and then she stopped. 'I really don't want to talk about it,' said Anna. 'I can't talk about it. I'm barely holding it together as it is.'

'But you are holding it together and you're probably the best shot we've got at this. You, me, and Justin are the only shot we've got at this, so keep holding it together,' said Kirsten. 'If you don't, I'll have to knock you back into shape.'

Anna flicked her eyes towards Kirsten. For a moment, Kirsten thought she was being scolded for being sharp with her. Then Anna nodded. 'Keep me in check.'

She turned and climbed into the lower bunk. Kirsten watched as she turned over to go to sleep. The train jerked as it did through most of the night, but Kirsten climbed the small ladder back up to the top bunk. She struggled to get back to sleep although she needed to, but when they arrived back in Inverness the following morning, she was ready to go. They took the car out towards Dores, parked up at Anna's house, and went to see Justin.

'Do you have anything yet?' asked Anna, strolling into the underground basement.

'No, it's quiet. It takes time to break in. I have to see patterns developing. There's a lot of data to pull for the smallest amount of evidence.'

'As quick as you can, Justin. Myself and Kirsten are off to Largs.'

The pair of them descended into a cupboard that Anna had in the basement. There were flashbangs, guns, and even a couple of grenades.

'Who are you expecting to be in Largs?' asked Justin, his eyes scanning the weapons.

'Godfrey; that's why we're going armed, in case anybody else has discovered him to be there as well.'

Justin gave a nod and then told them, 'Good luck.'

They were out of Dores before eleven, but the run to Largs took a good part of the day and it was late evening when they arrived.

The caravan park was on the north side of Largs, a bit out from the town centre. The holiday town was out of season and therefore a lot of the normal shops were empty though open, especially the chippies and cafes. But the area was not as busy as it could have been.

They drove up north along a road that hugged the coast and which was bombarded with speed restrictions and tight bends. Kirsten looked a little bemused. *Godfrey, here. You couldn't see it. You just couldn't see it. He'd be out in the country somewhere.*

'That's exactly why he's here,' said Anna, reading her thoughts. 'Nobody would think Godfrey would be here and in a caravan park, of all places.'

Kirsten drove up to the caravan park and found the gates closed. Would there be anybody up there? Rather than open the gates and drive in, Kirsten parked down at the roadside. The women stepped out of the car. It was a chilly evening, but Kirsten followed the path and then jumped over a fence inside the caravan park. In her tight leather jacket and black trousers, she could easily fade into the shadows. Anna joined her in similar garb.

'He said it was up near the back, but we can't trust that. I think we just start at the bottom and work our way up. Try to keep out of sight.'

'Is there going to be anybody here, though?' asked Kirsten. 'After all, it is out of season. I guess some people are, maybe people that own their caravan. You can't keep people away from it just because it's not holiday season, just because the rentals aren't being done.'

The pair worked up the steep slopes, checking every caravan. They looked inside. There were a lot of dark areas, but they also broke in, checking each caravan thoroughly. It took them several hours and by the time they'd finished, it was getting close to nine o'clock.

They wandered back down through the caravan park, almost sure that they would not find Godfrey. Kirsten saw that the small shop was open. 'I'm just going to pop in here for something,' she said.

Anna nodded and Kirsten entered a small shop stuck in a larger building. The rest of the building was closed off, but the shop wasn't. She entered through the door, which rang a bell, and found herself a chocolate bar. She was hungry and needed the calories. Around another small aisle, she found the counter to pay for her goods.

There was an old man in front of her, bent over. He had a hat on his head and a raincoat wrapped up tight. She thought nothing of it and the man turned away. Kirsten put the chocolate bar down and handed over some money. Something was annoying her, though. Something then clicked in her head.

The old man; he had sunburn towards the back of the neck, except the sunburn was at the bottom. The bare neck at the top was whiter. Why would you get a suntan like that? Unless it wasn't. Could the old man be wearing makeup? When she approached, he never turned and said hello. He never turned back. The whole way out, he kept his face from her.

Kirsten bolted from the shop. Anna Hunt was standing outside.

'Did you see the old man?' asked Kirsten.

'Yes, there was an old man who came out. Down those steps.'

'That's Godfrey,' said Kirsten.

'I'll get the car,' shouted Anna.

Kirsten started bolting down steps. With the caravan park on such a steep hill, everywhere you went either involved a climb or a descent or working along a path with one foot lower than the other. There were rows and rows of white caravans. Rows and rows of lightless caravans.

Kirsten ran down the steps the old man had gone. She slowed and crept along, wondering where he had gone. Time was ticking. As she got to the bottom, she heard a car start up. She looked over and saw one pulling away from a parking space. She ran in front of it, withdrawing her gun. It drove straight at her, forcing her to jump out of the way.

She saw Anna Hunt's car racing up from below and waved at it, pointing to the other car. Rather than jump in with Anna, Kirsten continued her descent. The road swept back and forward, but the path was going straight down, which meant that it crossed over the road every now and again.

Kirsten would run down, see the escaping car go past, and would clear the road just in front of Anna Hunt as she raced after it. Anna had come up a different road and now was descending after the fugitive car.

At about the fourth bend, there was a longer straight, and as she ran down the hill, Kirsten could see Anna Hunt overtaking the car and then pulling in front of it. The road was quickly coming down to the park exit. From her vantage point, Kirsten could see Anna slide her car in front. The other car collided with it. The car spun, and the gate at the front was smashed to smithereens. There was no movement from Anna Hunt's car.

149

The other car turned over and rolled several times.

Yet the old man stepped out and ran. Kirsten legged it down towards where the old man was running. Then she heard sirens. Some officer had obviously been near the scene. Flashing blue lights were almost there.

Kirsten changed track and ran straight to Anna Hunt's car to pull her out. As she put her arm around Anna's neck and pulled her to safety, a police officer shouted at Kirsten, telling her to stand still.

'I'm getting her clear. The thing could blow,' said Kirsten.

There was no sign that the car could blow up. The police officer obviously believed her, though, and began backing away. Kirsten looked at the groggy Anna Hunt, who simply gave her a nod.

'I'll need to talk to you two,' shouted the police officer.

Kirsten had taken Anna to the other side of the car. The officer clearly would not come past the car in case it blew up. Kirsten quickly grabbed their bags from the car and disappeared off into woods without looking back. Once there, she and Anna opened up, running as best they could. Soon they were out of sight, holed up in someone's back garden.

'Damn it,' said Anna. 'Damn it.'

'He's on foot too, though,' said Kirsten. 'We need to search. He could be anywhere around Largs or the nearby area.'

The pair split up. They were carless now. Anna would head north for at least four miles before turning back. Kirsten would go four miles south and through Largs. Anna would meet her somewhere in Largs and if they had no success, they'd find somewhere to stay.

Kirsten started making the trek south, but she didn't use the main road. The police would look for the two women who had caused the accident at the caravan park. She wasn't worried about the car. It was held in Service records. If the police checked it, that's what would come up. It would be discounted, pushed to one side. It would be recorded as a traffic accident. That was all.

It bothered her because the counter-Service may see that they had been there. They may follow. As Kirsten plodded along, the dark of the night was interrupted only by the occasional street lamp. Around the twisty corners down to Largs, she could see no one. In Largs, she wandered streets back and forth.

It was quaint enough, she thought. *The view out to the firth was impressive.* Godfrey could have gone north and gone away. He could have gone on a ferry over to one of the islands. He could have gone south into the town, caught a taxi, and be anywhere. They'd lost him.

Kirsten looked at the accommodations around her and decided that Godfrey was as good as gone. She strode into a hotel and asked for a twin room. Out of season, it wasn't a problem. She paid the bill and then she messaged Anna Hunt on her phone. It took Anna another hour and a bit to get back to the hotel, by which time Kirsten was sitting in the bar.

Anna walked in with wet hair, a shower having passed through half an hour ago. She undid her jacket, placed it over a chair, and sat there with Kirsten.

'That's that then.'

'Seems like it,' said Anna. 'It wasn't clever, was it?'

'I should have picked him out,' said Kirsten.

'I should have driven him off the road. He had a driver, for goodness' sake. He didn't drive that often.'

Kirsten looked over and pointed to an old whisky she saw

hanging up. She indicated she needed two doubles. The man behind the bar nodded before putting them in front of the women. As they sat there, a man came down into the bar. He was apparently on his own, and, first, looked around, scanning who else was in there. There was a couple, an old man, an older woman, and a husband and wife, from the looks of it. Otherwise, Kirsten and Anna were the only ones there.

He walked up to the bar and sat down beside them. He looked down at their drinks.

'On the good stuff, ladies,' he said. 'Out here in business myself. Came across in the Jag.' Kirsten had to stop herself from laughing. 'On my ownsome tonight. You girls stuck out here too?'

'Just having a drink,' said Kirsten.

'I'll buy you one.' He waved at the bartender, indicating that he should make three doubles. Kirsten put her hand over her whisky. 'What about your mother?' he said.

Anna Hunt stood up, walked around Kirsten, and put her hand up the back of the man's neck.

'Her mother's feeling good,' Anna said.

She bent down and kissed the man. Kirsten watched as the man's face took on a look of pleasure before he suddenly yelped. Anna Hunt withdrew, and the man's lip was bleeding. She'd actually bitten him.

'Mother's got a bit of bite. She plays with men, not with the boys. Come on, child of mine,' she said to Kirsten.

Kirsten had to stop herself from laughing out loud as she followed Anna Hunt off to their room. When she saw Anna open the door, she laughed, smiling at her. Anna's face was anything but happy.

'That's what I'm left with?' she said. 'That's what I'm left with. Mother? For the record,' said Anna, 'that's not the guy I want to spend my next forty years with. Don't care if he has a Jag.'

Chapter 19

'We blew it,' said Anna in the shower room. Kirsten could hear the water falling, as it had been for the last twenty minutes. *What was the woman doing in there? The rest of us want a shower as well*, Kirsten thought.

'Question is, where is he going to run to next?'

'No, it's how we blew it. I can't believe we didn't cut him off better. We had him. Now, we're going to have to chase again and all we've done is highlight him to other people. There's no point other people finding him first. If our plan is to use him as bait, then we need to be on top and in control, not just simply flushing him out.'

Kirsten knew this. Kirsten was well aware of what they had to do. Anna didn't need to go over it. That was the trouble with the twin room of the hotel. It was too small, you couldn't get space away. You didn't have time to stew in your own juices. Instead, someone was right in your face. And Anna, when she was annoyed, was not a great person to share a room with.

On top of all that, the laptop was open in front of Kirsten on the small desk that came with the room. The picture on the screen was of another room and a man with his back to them. Justin Chivers didn't like to have a camera on his face unless he was actively talking to you, so brief calls meant you got to see Justin. Longer efforts like this, where he was part of a general discussion in the room, meant she got to see Justin's back. That meant you forgot he was there. Maybe that was what he wanted. Maybe that was the reason he did it. Kirsten nearly jumped every time he said something.

Anna emerged from the shower with a towel wrapped around her head and another one around her body. She walked in front of the bed, took the towel off around her body, and began drying herself down.

Kirsten coughed. Anna turned suddenly, looked at the screen, and threw the towel back around her. 'Not that he's going to enjoy the view anyway,' said Anna.

'What's that?' said Justin. He was currently engaged in his computer screens, tapping away on his keyboard, but Kirsten wasn't sure what at. In fact, since he joined in the conversation an hour and a half ago, he had said little. The few words he had said had been jumped on by Anna.

They had slept in fits and starts. At one point, both of them were awake. They didn't start a discussion; sleep was required. They needed to be ready for the next bit, wherever that took place, whenever. Being a good operative was about knowing when to rest as well.

It had been a reasonably long campaign. They'd been out to Russia. They'd come back now, down to London, back up to Scotland, and then off to the west coast and Largs. It took its toll. You needed to grab what rest you could, when you could; sleep as best you could.

Anna had moved off to the side of the laptop, out of view, before she continued to dry herself, and Kirsten took the opportunity to get into the shower.

'Where else is there on that list?' said Anna. 'Where else would he go?'

'If indeed he's gone to any of them,' shouted Kirsten from the shower. 'We spooked him once already at his hidey-hole. Maybe he'll bin them. Maybe he'll start afresh.'

'Then we'll never get him,' said Anna. 'He's too smart to give his location away by spending a credit card here or there. He'll use cash all the way or have an account we don't know about. He's too darn good.'

'No, he's not,' said Kirsten from the shower. 'He's not because he let them in under his watch. The Service was compromised, and it happened on his watch.'

'Happened on my watch, too,' said Anna.

'No, it didn't. He was in charge. He knew everything; you didn't.' There were mutterings from outside and Kirsten knew she wouldn't be able to convince Anna of anything except she had failed. She tipped her head back, let the water run down through her hair, then took a squirt of shampoo and washed.

When Craig and she had left the Service, they'd stopped in a hotel, something like this, on the way out to Zante. She'd woken up that morning doing her hair just as she did now, but it had been different. Someone had joined her. Her mind cast back to that time. They were good times, carefree times, getting to Zante, getting into the sun.

The accommodation they'd rented. She'd actually started making connections with some locals. They'd thought about staying there, most days being warm, and a beach to sit on. For the few months they'd been there, it had seemed idyllic. Of course, they weren't sure what they would have done long term, but blending in, being a nobody, was good. Maybe it was only good because you had a somebody with you.

The lather having rinsed from her hair, Kirsten switched off the shower, stepped out, and dried herself within the shower room. When she stepped out with her towel around her looking for her clothing, Anna Hunt was already dressed. She was brushing her hair and Kirsten could see her almost shaking.

'Do you want me to do it?' she said. Anna turned and looked at her.

'Yes, yes. It's just that when I was in there, when they were—well, taking what they shouldn't have—he kept running his hands through my hair. He kept talking about my hair. I'm sitting looking in the mirror now, hating my hair.'

'I know plenty of fifty-year-old women who would die for hair like this,' said Kirsten.

'No, you don't,' said Anna. 'How many fifty-year-old women do you know?'

'Well, you.'

'Well, I did nearly die for it,' said Anna.

Kirsten didn't take up the conversation. She brushed Anna's hair, trying to smile as much as she could at the woman without looking like some demented, happy fool. Times were tough at the moment, really tough. Anna had been through an awful ordeal. Justin was still limping, and the odds weren't looking great. That wasn't what the woman needed right now. She needed built up. She needed cared for—something Kirsten did not expect.

Anna had been the rock, the very ideal of an exemplary operative. She knew her own mind, yet she also knew how the system worked. She could play it. Often, she was one step ahead.

But Kirsten remembered that feeling. That feeling of sheer helplessness when one of the greatest horrors that could happen to you was about to happen. Anna had saved her. Anna had stepped in and taken out those who had wished to do such things to Kirsten, and Kirsten hadn't been there for Anna. Yes, she'd saved her. Yes, she'd given her escape. Given her a way back to what she knew. But she hadn't been there when it mattered. She felt she'd let the woman down.

'Where have you gone?' asked Justin across the laptop.

Kirsten leaned to one side so that her head came into view. She tilted the laptop round so that Justin could see Anna and Kirsten. The man cut a bemused face at first.

'You realise I'm working very hard in here,' he said. 'I'm actually tailing down leads, working out where Godfrey is while you two seem to have some sort of beauty treatment.'

'Shut up,' said Anna. There was a silence in the room. Justin looked a bit bemused, and then he suddenly got it and stopped. He waited.

'Sorry,' said Anna. 'Sorry, it's just she's doing one of the nicest things that has been done for me lately.'

'I know,' said Justin. 'It's okay. It's me. Shouldn't have said it. Sorry. Do you want me to take a moment or to go on?'

'What have you got?' asked Anna.

'The car that Godfrey crashed was a rental which you would think would be quite easy to pick up. It wasn't, but I have, and it comes from a backstreet garage in Glasgow. They don't have many cars, so I reckon it might be somewhere that Godfrey would use on a necessary basis. Somewhere where you wouldn't be easily traced. However, they have recently rented out another one. In fact, the place has only rented out two cars in the last couple of weeks. The names are different.

I've run the registration plate through the automatic number plate recognition and the AMPR has got some movements.'

'How do you know it's him, though?' asked Kirsten. 'It could be anybody else in the other car. Maybe he's not gone to them; maybe he's gone to someone else.'

'Both cars were rented before Godfrey's crash with you. The other car was kept in Glasgow, except now it's moved. I followed a trail of number plate cameras and it's gone to Skye. There's an address in Skye on Godfrey's list.'

'Where was it?' asked Anna.

'Snizort,' said Kirsten. 'Snizort, he's gone to Skye, he's gone to Snizort. We could get a car and be up there in what, two, three hours? All we've got to do is head up into Glasgow, take the west road out through Kyle of Lochalsh and onto Skye. It won't take us that long.'

'Skye it is, then,' said Anna. 'Nice work, Justin. Monitor the cameras and that car. Can't be a coincidence; it's him. It must be where he is holed out, but we'll be careful when we go. We'll get up into the general area, but I don't want to rush into this like we did this time. We need to be watching him, be prepped for it. Make sure when we take him, we take him properly. We can't screw it up again because if we do, he'll know we have the list. It won't just be a chance sighting, it won't be us tailing him. It will be his list breached and he will go to somewhere completely different and we'll never find him.'

Kirsten put the hairbrush down, strode across to find her clothes out of her bag, and threw them on the bed. She went to put them on and then looked at the laptop in front of her. Justin was there, but he wasn't staring at her through the screen. Instead, his eyes were down, only occasionally looking up, his phone in front of him.

'It'd be best if we found somewhere,' he said, 'long before Snizort, travelling for your ops. If you're bedding down for the night anywhere, keep it well clear in case he's checking.'

'Good idea,' said Anna. She stood up, turned the laptop back, so it was square on the table, instead of being twisted round to her, and then caught Kirsten's look.

'Sorry, Justin, I just can't get used to that. Feel like I'm on some sort of dodgy website.'

Justin looked up and shook his head. 'And with a reputation like mine,' he said, but Kirsten had spun the laptop around so he was looking at the wall.

Anna was laughing.

'What?' asked Kirsten.

'The things we have to do, the situations we get ourselves in. I know in the past you've had to be in a very compromised position and yet you've got Justin there. A man less interested there could not be.'

'She made me face the wall,' he said. Kirsten shook her head at them and got changed.

Anna was already on her phone looking at Snizort and the surrounding area. She started pulling up OS Maps and looking at terrain and the rather limited address for where Godfrey was. They would have to search, or they would have to wait, let him move about. The two women went down to breakfast, planning on setting off as soon as they'd finished. They tried not to look like operatives, instead sitting in their trousers and t-shirt tops, but they were quiet.

'There's something bugging you, isn't there?' said Anna. 'When you did my hair, every now and again you would stop. It wasn't like you were working through it; you were thinking about something.'

'I don't get you,' said Kirsten, putting down her breakfast coffee. She went to put her hands down, but the white plate she'd eaten breakfast from was still there. She dropped her elbows on the table, put her hands together, and put her chin on it. Kirsten looked at Anna for a moment, then looked away.

'I didn't get you. When it was happening to me, you came for me. You saved me. I didn't save you from it. I see what it's done to you.'

'And you blame yourself,' said Anna. 'You blame yourself for what they did to me. What he did to me. Don't,' she said. 'If it wasn't for you, I'd have been getting the same treatment elsewhere, and maybe something worse. Who knows?'

'Godfrey was with Lorraine Hurst. He just dumped her. Didn't come back for her. He let her be tortured. He let her be turned. You came back for me. As did, Justin. I like to think that's what makes us different. I like to think that while we're running around and we have to despatch people, I like to think there is something, some sort of decency, that bonds us. It's a dirty world we work in, but some of us are not it. Some of us just have to step into it. I used to think that of Godfrey, but not anymore.'

'Did you really love him?' asked Kirsten, 'or was it just an infatuation? He being the experienced officer and . . .'

'I don't know,' said Anna. 'The thing is that, at that age, you've got so much more—is it romance—in you, so much more passion, drive. I look back at it now, and I know the feelings were intense, but I find it hard to actually say what they were. The important thing is, I know him for what he is now. This is about the Service. This is about our country. It isn't about Godfrey. It's just sometimes, I have to keep reminding myself of that.'

Chapter 20

The road to Skye, once they cleared Glasgow, was a stunning one. Despite the bad weather, Kirsten drank in the views as she drove along. She tried to point the odd thing out to Anna Hunt, but Anna was in a world of her own, and Kirsten wasn't sure what was bugging her. Was it the fact that she was having to face her feelings for Godfrey? The fact they were maybe still there? Or was it the horror that had happened back in Russia? Kirsten couldn't change either, so she continued to drive and lift the mood as best she could when she could.

The pair found a hotel in Kyle of Lochalsh. They checked in quickly before getting into the car and making their way out towards Snizort. Snizort was small, with various houses, all a little detached from each other. The area, in summer, may have been quite busy. Now that they were heading into winter, there was less of the tourist crowd making their way across the iconic bridge to Skye. There used to be a ferry. Indeed, the ferry had been the only way to get there, but times had changed, and there was now a large bridge. Had the bridge ruined the island?

One of the funny things about the Scottish Islands, thought

Kirsten, *was that the beauty of them was the remoteness.* She remembered her time on Lewis, which didn't have a bridge connection. Instead, you had to get the ferry. There were still plenty of tourists in the summer. Yet, because there were only two ferry sailings a day, as well as the other normal traffic that would be part of it, you ended up with only a certain number of tourists. Some locals said it was too many. Some thrived on the business they brought. Others complained about motorhomes.

Here, on Skye, there were no such restrictions. It flooded in the summer. Kirsten wasn't sure if she'd have wanted that to happen when she was on Lewis. Yet tourists brought money. It was one dilemma of the islands.

The pair parked up over two miles away from Snizort and walked across fields with their backpacks and binoculars, checking for signs of Godfrey. He may have been checking for signs of them. They kept low, using the small hillocks to their advantage. At the moment, this was strictly recon. Identify him, make sure he was there. After that, they'd decide how to proceed.

They arrived in the afternoon, and it was getting dark. They'd spent three hours lying on their bellies looking for Godfrey, and crawling to this point and that point. If he was there, he hadn't ventured out of any building he was in. Now, as darkness fell, the pair would make a proper assessment by getting close to the buildings.

There were few lights, and with an overcast sky, the darkness was intense. Their eyes really had to become accustomed. Any bright light shone at them meant they were looking into the dark, seeing no trace of an object for at least the next twenty seconds.

Slowly, they crept up on the first house. Kirsten moved under the main window, listening in as best she could. There was a TV, but no conversation. She spun away, faced along the side of the wall, and saw the light of the kitchen at the rear of the house. A blonde woman was making dinner. There were kids running about.

This wouldn't be a place for Godfrey. He didn't endanger civilians; didn't bring them into potentially lethal conflicts. He may have needed a nasty piece of work, but that wasn't Godfrey.

They spun on to the next house and saw a rather romantic couple in the living room. It was twenty houses later before they finally clocked him. The giveaway was the car they hadn't been able to see. He had parked it cleverly between the outbuilding and the house. You had to come up his drive to see it.

Anna had taken point on this one, and she was looking in through a crack in the window. The curtains had been drawn, but at the bottom, they were slightly askew. Godfrey was there, sitting with a glass of whisky, staring at a screen. The view didn't afford Anna a way of knowing what he was looking at. They'd done what they'd come to do. They'd found him.

Anna indicated they should retreat. It took half an hour to get back to the car. As they sat inside and started it up, Anna flipped the heating. It wasn't a normal thing for her. Kirsten was noticing she was feeling the chill more. Really out of sorts. *It could be the trauma*, thought Kirsten. *Everything could be the trauma.*

That was the trouble. The woman needed a proper assessment. She needed to get treatment and help. But she couldn't. She really couldn't until the game was up.

Kirsten reckoned they wouldn't win this game without Anna. For all the experience that Kirsten had, Anna was the wiser woman, the older woman, damaged or not.

They drove back to their hotel room, gave Justin a call, and told him they'd discuss in about an hour's time what they would do. The women made it downstairs for some dinner, but there was little conversation between them. When they returned up to the room, Kirsten flipped on the laptop. Making sure they were connected to Justin, Kirsten sat down on the bed, waiting for Anna. She'd disappeared into the bathroom, and when she'd come back out, Kirsten thought she saw red marks underneath her eyes. Her face was also wet. She'd been trying to wash or clean to some description.

'You okay?' asked Kirsten. Anna gave a nod, almost dismissively, but then she stopped.

'No, but there's no time to discuss that. When we're done, we take care of that. Right now, we've found him. He's unaware that we've found him.'

'Are you sure? Are you sure he hasn't got some sort of device watching us? On his perimeter?'

'I'm sure,' said Anna. 'We need to make sure that he stays here or else we lift him.'

'What are we trying to do?' asked Justin. 'We're trying to use Godfrey as bait. If we grab him, that will not happen. He won't accept being used as bait. He'll do everything in his power to resist us, to get clear again, to be out on his own, and to protect those secrets. His beef is in stopping that bunker being infiltrated and also in keeping himself safe from a woman coming after him, who frankly wants to kill him and all his work. I think kidnapping him is going to put us under tremendous pressure,' said Justin.

'But if we get him, we can take him up to this anti-Service group. We could take him in as an offering. That way, we could get through to them, get through to the head people and close it down. It's violent, but it's fast,' said Kirsten.

'No,' said Anna. 'It's too violent, too fast. Something goes wrong, we lose. We said we would ambush them, and ambush them we shall. But we need to bring them to Godfrey. We need to get on the inside. There's no way they're going to see me as turning. I've got no reason to turn. They'll look back through my history. It's with Godfrey.

'If anything, I'm going to fall on his side. There is no history of Godfrey betraying me. There is no public knowledge of it, so there's no way they'll trust that I've turned. It's me; it's Anna. I was practically his lieutenant. I was the one he went to. Nobody's going to believe that I'm bringing him in for them.'

'It has to be you, Kirsten,' said Justin.

'Me?'

'Of course, it does,' said Justin. 'It has to be you. Craig, you've gone after Craig. You've gone looking for Craig, torn between him and the Service. The monster the Service is becoming will be your beef. You've seen what Godfrey's done to it.'

'It's not what Godfrey's done to it; it's what they've done to it. The Service has been the same all the time,' said Kirsten.

'You know that. I know that. They don't know that's how you feel. You can go into turmoil. You have got a heck of a justification to bring Godfrey to them. Also, you are capable of doing it on your own, and that's key. It all sits; it all works.'

'Listen to him,' said Anna. 'Craig's the way in. You need to contact Craig. Tell him you have a contact for Godfrey. Don't tell him you have Godfrey. Tell him you can find him. It's what they want. It's what she will want. Gethsemane wants Godfrey.

Yes, the Russians want to bring this down. They want to rip the whole service up, but Gethsemane's beef is with Godfrey in particular. She needs to get him face to face. She also needs that for her masters, because they want that information, and only Godfrey knows where it is.'

'Just a moment,' said Kirsten. 'One thing I don't like about this is how it puts Godfrey into their hands. We could hand them all this information.

'Of course. Absolutely, it can. That's the game. That's the ploy. It's how we bring them in. We need a big fish. We need a massive hook,' said Anna. 'You need to do this.'

'An ambush doesn't work,' said Justin, 'unless people think they are safe, unless people are content with what's going on. You're going to have to be good. You're going to have to convince Craig. He can sell it to the others, but you're going to have to sell it to him.'

'What? How long will this take? I'm going to need to get to Craig, first. He's broken ties with me. The last time he turned away from me on the bridge, he went back to them. I begged him. I was on my knees.'

'Yet he reached out to you,' said Justin. 'That means he wants a reunion. He wants you.'

'But he wants me on their terms, to be with them.'

'That's because he's fallen on that side,' said Anna. 'That works for us. Don't trust who Craig is now. Don't trust that this will all work out fine. You and Craig will probably still blow up. He is gone, but he has to believe you're not. He has to believe that divide isn't there anymore, that for some reason you're wanting him. You need him more than all of this put together. He has to believe that Kirsten Stewart wants to be Craig's.'

167

'Okay, but what do we do in the meantime? I can't make this happen tomorrow,' said Kirsten.

'In the meantime, I watch Godfrey,' said Anna. 'Justin helps you from a distance and I watch Godfrey so that if he moves, we know where to go. I won't lose him. I have worked too damn hard to get to the man this time. Sacrificed too much. We need to clean up this country. We need to clean up this Service. I am in it until it's resolved or until I'm no more,' said Anna. 'I hope you are too. I know it's going to be tough for you. Trust me, I know. But you're made for this. You're made to operate under the extreme circumstances. Trust in what you do and do it well.'

Kirsten nodded. Justin asked for the all-agreed. 'I'll head up to Dores then,' said Kirsten. 'Join up with you, Justin. We'll sit and plan this properly, see what else I need to get in. I'll head up tonight.'

The call was closed down to Justin, and Kirsten made sure she had all her belongings.

'Take the car,' said Anna. 'I'll get another one. That won't be a problem and it will look better if it's a hired car from somewhere around here. Less suspicious.'

Kirsten nodded and went to leave the room, but Anna stopped her.

'Listen,' she said. 'Us sisters, we've got to stick together. I know what we're asking you to do is hard. It's hard beyond belief. The last thing you want to see is Craig in the middle of this. If he isn't coming back, the ambush is going to be as much for him as for Gethsemane. But you're tough and you can do it.'

Anna put her arms around Kirsten, pulling her close. 'We need each other, need each other to get through this. We started out as a three,' she whispered into her ear, 'we're still a three. Still a partnership to the end.'

Kirsten leaned back away from Anna. 'To the end. Until we bring it down and the Service stands again or until we fall.' Kirsten stepped away. 'You know when that guy said you were my mom?'

Anna looked at her, wondering what was coming.

'I was okay with that comment.'

Kirsten said no more, put her bag on her shoulder and walked out of the room. She was heading towards what was probably the most difficult time of her career, maybe of her life. It had all become personal again. Craig at the middle. Was he saveable? Kirsten had to admit to herself, she so hoped so; she truly hoped so. She did still have something in there for him.

Chapter 21

Kirsten arrived at Dores and was greeted by Justin in Anna Hunt's small abode. They sat together in the kitchen, cup of coffee in hand, musing about how to get the job done.

'If we want to get to Craig, it will not be easy,' said Justin. 'He's Service. He's an operator. He knows how to keep his nose clean. We were lucky with Godfrey. We got a heads-up, but we also worked beside Godfrey. Anna was as close to Godfrey in the Service as anyone. That's why she knew the surrounding figures. We are also lucky that George helped. He could see the danger.

'We will not get that with Craig. They're on the opposite side. He may be difficult to reach, especially as they won't want people to find him. Their entire goal will be Godfrey, finding him. Therefore, they'll want minimal distraction elsewhere. The Service is a mess. That bit of their job is done.'

'If we can't come at Craig directly,' said Kirsten, 'then maybe we could get someone who could get hold of Craig, someone who has worked with him in the past. Could you trace Mark Lamb? Do you think we could get a way in there?'

'Possibly,' said Justin. 'Possibly. Let me see what previous intel had on him.'

Justin walked through to the living room, where he sat down in front of his laptop. Kirsten came through, watched him for a few moments, and realised that this was going to take a while. She walked out and down to the beach on the shores of Loch Ness at Dores.

It wasn't a beach like they had in Zante, where you could lie in the sun. She enjoyed that with Craig. She'd lay there; every now and again he would get up, turn around and stare at her. Occasionally, he'd bend down and give her a kiss, maybe a cuddle. They had been good times, the world out of the way and just the pair of them. That wouldn't be the case anymore, though.

She took a stone and skimmed it across the water, watching as it bounced two, three, four, and then a fifth time before it went 'plop'. *Is that what the Service was like?* she thought. *You jump across the water until finally you sink beneath it.*

Kirsten turned, walked back to where she saw a large rock, and sat down. She was worried about where this could go, what position she could be put in with Craig. Everyone kept telling her to let go of him. He's turned, forget him, but if he was turned, she couldn't forget him because he would be a danger. Even without his legs, Craig was still an operator, could still find a way. He could still handle a gun.

She sat there, musing at the water with the grey clouds above. She would've loved to have been like Nessie, the legendary monster of the Loch, hiding away from everyone. Barely seen—everybody wanted him. Nobody could find him. When this was all over, that sounded good, away and having no one to think about, no one to worry about. Lie on a beach somewhere. Maybe she'd even find a man to come and share that with her.

Maybe she just needed the solitude for a while.

Uruguay would have been nice. Uruguay would be good to visit again, but with no connotations. No job to do. Just plenty of water, beaches, good food, maybe even the odd bar, a risky affair. She laughed. When did Kirsten ever have affairs?

Maybe she should. Maybe that's what she needed in her life. She'd never been a great one for relationships, but prior to her brother dying, she had spent so much time looking after him. That had been enough. He wasn't a hassle, but he took time. All that he wasn't and the lack of understanding he had about the world, he was one person who would truly hold her, giving her love without conditions. Someone just truly happy to see her. She missed him. She really missed him.

It was an hour or two later when Kirsten made her way back to the house, and as she came through the door, she saw Justin turn his head and smile. He had something; that was his way. If he had got nothing, his head would've been down in the computer, ignoring her. But he had something.

'Spill it,' she said.

'Spill it? Is that it? No "please?"'

He was teasing now. 'Just tell me, Justin,' she said.

'I've been looking into some records that some of our police friends have. At the moment, they're currently keeping eyes on certain Irish connections to Mark Lamb. He's needing some more material for his work, and a lot of that material seems to ferry through Ireland via old dissidents. I know that one company they have been monitoring is Yellowbrickland Transport.

'Yellowbrickland Transport operates out of Belfast. Legitimate company, but there have been rumours and connections that it is moving items across the Irish sea. Mark Lamb has been mentioned. There's no guarantee about when shipments are happening, but there was a rumour that tomorrow there is something going on. I've cross connected that with something the Service picked up previously.

'The driver that's coming across tomorrow, Ian Brown, has got a tag against him by the Service for moving bomb-making equipment. I've checked, and he's not a consistent driver for Yellowbrickland Transport either. He's an on-hire, a worker they pick up from another firm, Transport Kings or something they're called. Anyway, they hire out people, these transport companies, to pick up extra jobs so the other companies don't have to keep large numbers of staff.

'Whenever Transport Kings does this for Yellowbrickland, Ian Brown is sent over. Of course, that all makes sense. You'd send the same guy, but every time—every single time—he is available, and these are the only times that Yellowbrickland Transport requests help? There's not enough proof. It's all very circumstantial, and that's why nobody is moving on it, but I think it's enough for us to move.'

'I think it is. Where's he routing then?' asked Kirsten.

'It's in the early morning. I think it's three o'clock, it's coming over. The slow ferry from Ireland. It'll take about four hours, get in around seven, or just after at Cairnryan. The shipment's meant to be heading for Stirling, so it'll head up towards Ayr. I think that's the place to act. I've tried to do a bit of digging into Ian Brown. The good news is, from what I can gather, he's quite the ladies' man.'

'What do you mean?'

'Well, his subscriptions to various websites would say he's very interested in women, especially the naughty kind.'

'You think he'd pick up a hitchhiker?' queried Kirsten.

'Well, if you can make yourself attractive,' said Justin. 'Never really seen the interest myself.'

Kirsten smiled at him. 'I think you're playing it both ways. A double bluff. I think you love the ladies,' she said.

'If only. It would have been a lot easier, especially in my early days. My father wouldn't have been so disappointed.'

'You're nobody's disappointment,' said Kirsten. 'But I will need to get some different clothing. I'm going to pop into Inverness, buy a few things. You think I could pass for a German tourist?'

Justin laughed. 'I swear this is the bit you like about this job,' he said. She grinned and turned to get the car.

That evening, Kirsten tried on her outfit. She wondered if it was too over the top. Maybe too obvious. But that's what she was doing, wasn't it? She was selling a dream to this man.

There was a pair of shorts which she felt were a size too small. She had boots that rolled up to just under the knee and a blouse that she tied in the middle instead of using the buttons. She braided her hair down her back and had a pair of glasses, so she looked quite academic. There was a backpack as well. That would contain the clothing she would change back into, as well as her weapons.

She had to leave that night, however, driving down and stopping at Stirling in a hotel. She was up the next morning early, for it would still be a couple of hours' drive to get to where she wanted to be.

On the outskirts of Ayr, just beyond the town of Minishant, Kirsten walked, heading towards Ayr. She listened intently, waiting to see if any lorries would pass by. Yellowbrickland Transport was what she was looking for. She didn't raise a thumb to any other, and then the rain came down, a heavy shower that soaked her to the skin.

As it finished, she turned to see more lorries coming and saw one that said Yellowbrickland Transport on it. She put her thumb out, turning to make sure that the driver could get a full view of her. He went past, but she saw him pull in further ahead. She turned and started running towards the large articulated lorry. As she did so, she realised he'd jumped out of the cab and was coming towards her. This was going better than she'd hoped.

'You look soaked through,' said the man.

'Yes,' said Kirsten, putting on as good a German accent as she could. 'I am, how you say it, soaked through. Yes?'

His eyes were everywhere, and he helped her up to the passenger side of the lorry. When she feigned difficulty in getting up the enormous step into the cab, the man put his hands on her backside, pushing her up and into the wagon. He was quickly round to the other side.

They drove along. Kirsten gave the impression she was cold. It wasn't difficult to do. The scant clothing she had on, combined with the soaking she received, had meant she was chilled.

'Is there anywhere we can stop, somewhere quiet?' she said. The man looked at her strangely. 'It's just I was soaked through. I need to take out my towel and dry myself. If we stop on the road, people might see. I want to dry properly and change.'

A smile went across the man's lips. Justin had got him perfectly. *A little pervert*, thought Kirsten. The man stopped less than half a mile further up the road, but he was able to pull the wagon off and into a long parking area, which currently had no other vehicles in it. There were trees on either side.

'Here's good,' he said. 'You could go outside, into the trees,

175

or, if you want, I'll put the heater on in the cab. Just change in here. I don't mind.'

'And you will go where?' asked Kirsten, continuing the German accent.

'It's only right and fair that I get to stay in my cab, isn't it? Or if you go out there, I could give you some assistance.'

The man had put his hand forward onto her thigh. He never saw the left hand swinging around, and she caught him with a punch right on the chin. She followed it up with another two.

The man was out cold. Only then did Kirsten take the towel from her bag, strip down, dry off, and change into the clothing she wanted. She was back in black, a baseball cap on her head, trying to look like a lady trucker.

Kirsten checked the mirrors and saw no one else in the layby. She tied the man up, pushing him down into the footwell on the passenger side of the cab. Taking the gun out of her bag, she placed it just inside her trousers.

Kirsten hadn't driven many articulated lorries, but it had been a requirement when she'd gone through training. You never knew what you would have to deal with. And if you're involved in the war against drug running, you may end up having to drive the evidence away or indeed take it back off the bad guys.

She turned the engine over, foot down on the accelerator, and worked her way steadily through the gears. The articulated lorry routed back out onto the main road.

Kirsten was heading for Sterling to an address that was on the manifest documentation sitting at the front of the cab. The man had already put the route into the sat nav, so the next couple of hours would be easy. There was, however, a stop off on the route.

Kirsten was almost enjoying herself as the articulated lorry arrived at Stirling. She drove past the city and then the sat nav had her take a left onto a minor road and then left again onto a country lane. There was then a runoff into a large farm area where a man was waiting. She pulled up and jumped down from the cab.

'Where's Mr Brown?' asked the man.

'Mr Brown, unfortunately, got ill. Debbie Brown, his daughter. How do you do?'

Kirsten put her hand over, and the man shook it.

'Shall we get this done?' he said. He was such a contrast to Ian Brown, whose tongue had practically been hanging out of his mouth when he saw her. This man was all business. When he looked at Kirsten, the eyes were looking for deceit, scanning for danger.

The man started walking towards the rear of the van. Kirsten followed him to where he cut a tag off the rear door. The tag was put around once a load had been secured. If it was broken, people would know the load had been interfered with. The man had a spare tag in his hand and handed it to Kirsten, along with the broken tag. The number on both was identical.

He pulled open the rear door of the lorry, jumped up inside, and made his way to a certain box which had a lock on it. He put the key in, opened the lock, took out what was inside, which seemed to be a small brown packet. The man closed the box, came outside, and closed the door.

'Put the tag back on it,' he said, 'or didn't your father tell you that?'

Kirsten pulled her gun out into the man's face.

'I haven't had a father for a long time,' said Kirsten. 'Mr Brown, however, was very helpful. I need to see Mark Lamb, and you're going to take me there directly, because that's where you're going with this stuff. You'll accompany me. If you don't, I'll kill you. If you vary along the route, I'll kill you. Try to warn anyone, I'll kill you. Just so you're aware of that.

'If you take me to Mark Lamb, I will let you live. He might kill you, but frankly, that's not on me. If you really want someone to blame, you can either blame Mr Brown for his rather perverted desires or Mr Lamb, because, frankly, he's been pretty slack in the way he's obtained these explosives.'

Chapter 22

The man went to a car with Kirsten holding a gun in his back. The car was red and sporty, and Kirsten indicated he should get inside, and she sat in the front seat with him.

'Where is Mark Lamb at the moment?'

'Perth,' he said. 'It'll be a brief drive, but not too far. Maybe we could dispense with the gun.'

'If we dispense with the gun and you do something silly, I have to attack you with what I've got. My hands are much more bloody. I'll tear you apart. The gun would be quicker and more preferable. Let's keep the gun,' said Kirsten. The man's face was impassive. He started the car and drove.

'Do you think I should warn him? If we turn up and you're in the car, he may just shoot us both.'

'He won't shoot us both.'

'I don't think it's advisable. But let's not let Mr Lamb get too excited. If he does, he might not make our rendezvous. Are you meant to send him a signal at all?'

'No,' said the man. 'You have, however, left the wagon of Mr Brown behind. That'll get found, eventually.'

'Indeed, it will,' said Kirsten, 'with Mr Brown tied up inside, surrounded by some rather excitable clothing from a German tourist.'

She was almost laughing at this; the ridiculousness of it. The man continued to drive along the A9 up towards Perth. At this time of day, the road was reasonably clear, and as they reached the large roundabout at Perth, he continued north. However, once the road had narrowed down from a dual carriageway into a single carriageway, the man pulled off the road. They were heading into what Kirsten now regarded as the true Highlands.

He didn't go far, though. Maybe two or three miles before he pulled off into a wooded glade to a house sat within. He stopped the car, and Kirsten saw men approaching with guns.

'I didn't call ahead,' said the man. 'This is what he does. It's standard.'

Kirsten held a gun to the man's head as the other men came to the door of the car and opened it. A face looked in.

'Let's not get excited,' said Kirsten, 'lest this man lose his head. I'm here to talk to Mark Lamb. I have a proposition for him.'

Of course, she didn't. All Kirsten wanted from Mark Lamb was a way to Craig. She would not give him anything for it; he just needed to do it.

'Let's step out of the car slowly then,' said the man. Kirsten nodded, opened her car door, and backed out, but her gun remained trained on her driver.

'Did you bring the package with you?' asked one guard.

'Yes,' said Kirsten, 'and I'll happily hand it over to Mr Lamb. I take it he is here. An item like this he'll want to inspect. Make sure it's what he wants.'

The guard turned to one man, told him to explain things to

the boss.

'Just wait out here,' said the man.

The driver remained in the car, so Kirsten didn't move away from her door, the gun still trained on her driver. The guard came back shortly and gave a nod to the guard in charge.

He looked at his fellow guards and gave them a nod. Their weapons were lowered. In return, Kirsten lowered hers.

'This way,' said the guard, and Kirsten walked behind him as he led her towards the house. The other guards followed, as well as the driver.

The house was relatively modern, and from a large window, Kirsten could see that Mark Lamb was sitting inside. He had a glass of wine on the table beside him. The guard led her in through the front door, down a hallway, and then opened the door into Mark Lamb.

'If you put the gun to one side, we can be much more civil about this,' said Lamb upon seeing her.

'Well, I'm not taking a drink from you,' said Kirsten.

Lamb laughed. 'Such a pity our rendezvous didn't go so well that night. I have to say, you're very impressive. Not just your looks, everything about you, the way you handle yourself. You got lucky that night, though. I saw you afterwards. They were going to hand you over. It wasn't my idea, but the other men were there. I heard you dealt with him. I left before all that happened.'

'If you don't mind, I'll not put my gun down,' said Kirsten. 'And anyway, if I did, as I told one of your colleagues, things would just be a lot bloodier. The result will still be the same.'

She sat down in a chair that gave her a view of the window, Mark Lamb, and everybody else in the room.

'I'll keep a couple of my boys in then, if you don't mind.'

'Of course not,' said Kirsten. 'How many can you afford to lose?'

Mark Lamb laughed again. 'You've certainly got a confidence about you, haven't you? But why do you want me? You know I'm not part of them. I'm a man that earns his money and then goes and enjoys it. If I can earn money off you, I'll gladly help, depending on what it is you're looking for.'

Kirsten took the package that had been in the articulated lorry and put it on a table beside her.

'That's what you were shipping. By the way, you may run things in a way that can't be prosecuted, or can't be acted on by the normal police, but you're really obvious in terms of moving things about.'

'I'll try to remember that. What is it you want from me?'

'I need you to set a meeting up with me and Craig; Gethsemane if necessary, but me and Craig.'

'Why?'

'Frankly, that's none of your business. The thing is though, and I'll tell you this for free because they'll ask you, Craig's right. Craig is right about the Service. I've been away; I've investigated. It's a mess. It's a mess created by Godfrey, and we need to turn it around. I'm in, and I need to tell him I'm in. I need to show them, so I have to find him.

'You'll have a way of getting to him because you're working with him. You probably have a phone somewhere, a contact, a drop. She watched the man's face. There was that flinch. She was right. 'For their introduction, I'll leave your bomb here with you. If I don't get an introduction, I might set it off.'

'You could try setting that one off, but it wouldn't work. It hasn't got the correct reagent with it, so that's not a threat I'm taking seriously. The other thing is that I value my contracts.

I've made good money out of them, these Gethsemane people. Very easy to work with. Say what they want, you deliver it, they pay the money. No messing about. The kind of people I like to do business with.'

'So, do business with me. They'll pay you. Craig will pay you for bringing me back into the fold.'

The man stood up and walked over to his men. He turned, put his hands together as a little triangle and then brought them up to rest his chin on them.

'It's a tempting offer. The thing is, my relationship with them is good. I am making plenty of money out of them. I trust them. Trust what they want and that they will pay to get it. You, I don't know what you want. You are on the other side. I've told you I was there when they hung you up, just before they made you fight. Just before they would've . . . well, rather unpleasant to do that to a lady.'

Kirsten felt sick to the core. Had he been the dark man in the room, had he been outside, had he watched? But she held those feelings in check. He was still the best way in.

'I value their custom. Taking you to them would be a risk. What do I get if you are genuine? A little money. What do I get if you're not? The ending of one of the most lucrative partnerships I've had in a long time. This is business, nothing else, so, no, I won't do it.'

'Very well,' said Kirsten. 'The bomb I can't set off. I guess that bit of intimidation is no longer available.' She stood up and began walking over to Mark Lamb. 'No hard feelings,' she said. 'I have other routes in. You're a man that knows his business, so I won't take up any more of your time. I won't threaten you. I won't make the mistake of trying something like that in your own place.'

She put her hand out, and he shook it. 'Business,' he said, 'just business.'

'Indeed.'

She turned and was immediately escorted by four of his guards. They opened the door and walked into the hallway.

Two steps in, Kirsten drove an elbow up into the face of the guard on her right-hand side. Before the next one could react, he was struck across the face. Those in front turned, raised their weapons, but Kirsten was able to grab the outer hand, drive them upward, and push them down to the ground. By the time they went to react, she had pulled her own handgun and had shot dead the two she had pushed to the ground.

Those behind her were still groggy, but she dispatched them on the way back to Mark Lamb. He was running for a cabinet inside the lounge. She closed the door behind her, continued to walk up to him.

He turned with a gun in his hand, but she grabbed his wrist, twisted it hard, causing him to drop the gun. She then butted him in the face, and he sprawled on the floor.

Stepping to one side of the room as the door opened, Kirsten turned, fired, and shot dead the man who had come in. She then turned and drove a kick down onto the jaw of Mark Lamb. He was out cold. She hurried to the door of the room, up the hallway to the front door, where she saw a rather panicked driver. He ran for the car.

'Don't,' she said. He continued. She dispatched two shots into him. Sighing as she put her gun away, she walked up to the body. Kirsten put two arms underneath him and dragged him back into the house and into the corridor where the rest of the bodies lay.

She then locked the front door and went inside. Pulling

Mark Lamb away into another room, she found a seat. She tied him up to it and then got a bucket of cold water before coming back into the room. She poured it over him. The man shook his head, tried to struggle, but couldn't break his restraints. He looked around for his men. Then he looked at her in terror.

'They're all dead. I lied about that bit, shaking of hands and that. You're going to take me to see Craig. You're going to tell me how you're going to do it. Then you're going to do every step precisely as described and we're going to meet Craig. If you do that, I won't kill you. If you deviate from the plan, I will.

'What Craig does is up to Craig. Maybe Gethsemane will step in and tell him to finish you, or maybe you're a good enough bomber that they need to hang on to you. When I was growing up, they said in school that you needed to get a skill; you needed to get something you could do. That way, people put value on you. And hats off, you've developed that skill. Few can blow people up the way you do.'

Kirsten stepped forward, putting her gun under the chin of Mark Lamb. 'And you blow up whatever; good people, bad people, you don't care, you're a mercenary. Personally, I'd rather see you dead,' she said. 'You deserve it for the terror you've put into this world, but I need to see Craig. You're going to take me. How?'

'No,' said Mark Lamb, 'I won't do it.'

'Understand this,' said Kirsten. 'You can do it. Take me to Craig and I will let you go. However, if you don't take me, I will kill you, but not before you beg me for death. I will hurt you. I will make you pay for every bomb that you've built. Understand?'

She reached forward, driving her thumb up and into his throat. He gurgled. Her nail drove into his skin. Blood ran out from the side. She pressed and pressed until he begged her to stop.

'That's nothing. I picked up skills as well. They train you to do stuff like this. I don't even like doing it, but I know it gets results, and that's why I'm going to do it, if you understand. Otherwise, let's see Craig.'

The man nodded. 'Go into the living room. Under the large pot, there's a phone there. Bring it through here. I need to talk to them, arrange where to meet.'

'Okay, but no funny business,' said Kirsten.

She retrieved the phone, brought it back into the room where Mark Lamb was being held.

'Dial the second number down, not the first one. First one's a decoy. It's what we do when something's been compromised.' Kirsten dialled the second one, held the phone up to Mark Lamb, but kept it on speaker.

'I need to see Craig,' he said simply when the phone was answered.

'Location 5,' said a voice.

The phone call was closed down as quickly as that.

'Don't think about using that one again,' said Mark Lamb. 'There are others around the house. That one is now gone. They won't accept any calls from that number. They'll see it as a red flag. If you check inside the vase that you found that phone under, there'll be a piece of paper and Location 5 will be on it.'

Kirsten walked back, put her hand down into the large vase, and pulled out a piece of paper. Indeed, Location 5 was in the Highlands. A grid reference, which she checked on her phone.

'Twenty-five-minute drive,' said Kirsten. 'They'll expect us then, within half an hour.' She cut the binds that held Mark Lamb. 'Don't mess me about,' she said.

The drive up was uneventful. Mark Lamb did the driving, Kirsten with a gun at his side as he drove further up the A9 before cutting off again, this time near to the House of Bruar. It was a little further down the road; another retreat sheltered away and the car pulled up the driveway.

Kirsten saw stone steps leading down from a large house. The house was old, but impressive, and certainly would have enough room to accommodate many people. She saw a few guards here and there, but she wasn't interested in them. The only person she was interested in, as she held a gun to Mark Lamb's head, was walking down the steps. At first, she had to look twice. Then she saw the strips. She'd seen paraplegics running in the Olympics with them, and now, before her very eyes, Craig was walking towards her, his damaged legs now extended.

Chapter 23

Craig continued down the steps. He tried to hide it, but Mark Lamb looked edgy in the car seat beside Kirsten. She told him to get out, and she exited the car on the passenger side. Part of Kirsten was amazed Craig had such balance on the . . . what did they call them? Were they limbs? They bent under his weight as he stepped down the steps, and she wondered how fast he could go on them. Were they just for walking about, or did he run on them?

They were different, after all. When she had seen them, they were used for running and sports. They were amazing, but strange too. Anyone who had prosthetic legs, they looked more normal. More like a leg. Less like a bendy piece of plastic or—she didn't have the words for it, her mind racing as she looked at Craig. Then he skipped down the last couple of steps at speed towards her before he stopped and scowled at Mark Lamb.

'What is she doing here?' he said.

'She's brought me here at gunpoint,' said Lamb. 'She's come to see you. You better ask her what it's about.'

'She better go and see Gethsemane then,' said Craig. 'Bring her.'

188

He turned and walked away up the steps, but Kirsten shouted after him.

'Bring her? Her? What's that meant to mean? This is me. You don't walk away from me!'

He continued, and she tore around the car, ignoring Lamb.

'I said you don't walk away from me.'

She grabbed his shoulder. He turned around and swiped at her. Kirsten was quick enough to duck out of the way as he was going to slap her.

'Do you know what it's taken me to get here? Do you?'

'It's taken the incompetence of that man over there,' said Craig, pointing at Lamb. 'She won't be happy with that.'

'And what are you happy with? Are you happy to see me?'

He scowled at her, and she let her face soften. Inside, she wasn't sure if she was acting or not. 'Craig, I've looked at him. I've looked into Godfrey. I'm not daft. When you said those things about him, when you said things about the Service, it wasn't that I didn't believe you, didn't trust you, but I needed to see things for myself. You had such a trauma. You had such a horror to go through. I needed to know if you were on the right track. You could have been so easily turned, so easily.'

'This is me,' he said. 'I won't lie down. I won't be something pathetic.'

'And look at you,' said Kirsten. 'Look at you.'

She reached forward, grabbed the back of his head, and kissed him. At first, he didn't respond. It was like kissing a statue, stiff lips, but then she felt hands go around her, pulling her close, driving his mouth towards hers. Then he slipped. Was it the limbs? Was he unused to this? She didn't know. He broke off at that point, almost angry with himself.

'So, what are you back for?'

'Because I've found him. I know where Godfrey is.'

'Well, if you were the same mind as us, why didn't you just kill him?'

'It's Godfrey. It's not that easy. We'll talk to your Gethsemane. She'll want to know as well, but I'm here for help. I'm here to sort the Service out.'

Craig stared into her eyes. His hand went round to the back of her head, pulling at the braided ponytail. 'That's different,' he said.

'It's a disguise. I had to interrupt one of Mark's explosive convoys. The man driving it, I think he liked women not wearing a lot with a visitor look about them. He thought I was German.'

'You can't do accents,' said Craig. 'Your accents are terrible.'

'I don't think it was the accent that was pulling him in.' She laughed a little. For a moment, Craig laughed back.

'Come on,' he said. He looked back towards Lamb. 'And you get your arse in here, too. She'll want to talk to you.'

Kirsten looked back and saw Mark Lamb's face. He was worried, deeply worried, but he trudged up the steps behind him.

It was a modern building, though it looked grand. The hall, inside the front door, was wide, light, and airy, with paintings on the walls. To Kirsten, it looked like somebody didn't know the difference between old and new, and they'd tried to ram both into the same place.

Craig took them onward, out to the rear, where there was a swimming pool, and beside it, a small bar. Sitting at a table beyond the bar was an older woman, possibly Anna Hunt's age.

'What's this you bring me?' asked the woman. The accent

was strange. There was a hint of Russian in there, but also something from the Black Country. Kirsten struggled to place it exactly.

'I haven't brought you anything,' said Craig. 'Kirsten has come back to us herself.'

'Really? She didn't trust you the first time round and now she's here.'

'She needed to see for herself,' said Craig. 'She's a doubting Thomas. Pretty normal in our line of work. When everything's falling apart, who do you trust?'

'She trusted you enough to have a look. That's very good. Come up here,' said the woman, waving to Kirsten.

Kirsten walked past Craig. He gave her a faint smile. 'Take a seat. Make her something, Craig. What does she drink?'

'Coffee,' he said.

'Then make her a nice coffee. I see Mr Lamb is here.' The woman's face changed, angry now. 'I'm wondering how you found us, my dear. My name's Gethsemane.'

'Your name,' said Kirsten, 'is Lorraine Hurst, and I understand why you don't like Godfrey. You're quite something. Escaping from Russia. Pulling off a retreat like that.'

'I think you're quite the same. I heard about your exploits in Uruguay, Argentina, London—twice in London, I believe.'

'That's just the job. You got away when you were held.'

'As did you, from some of our associates. Nasty bit of business, that. I have to say, Craig here wasn't happy when he heard about it. I don't blame him. It's a terrible weapon to use on someone, but such are the people we have to work with.'

'I've seen what Godfrey's doing. I've talked to many people now, seen the worst of it. The hard bit has been coming back to find you.'

'Easy enough,' she said, looking at Mark Lamb.

'But I found Godfrey. Anna Hunt was looking for him, too. I worked with her for a bit. Anna knows Godfrey from old, as I believe you do,' said Kirsten.

It was a tough act to portray. She couldn't come across as completely naïve, as if she'd suddenly been sold on the cult of Gethsemane. Also, the woman needed to believe her, believe that she was now invested in righting the Service. There could be no hint of undermining it, destroying it. This had to be about a vendetta against Godfrey.

'You've certainly done your homework, but you say you know his whereabouts.'

'I do,' said Kirsten, reaching out with her hands as a coffee was brought to her. She sniffed it. It was good. It had been made properly, a quality to it. As she looked around, she saw there was a quality to everything. Even the drinks that were at the bar weren't the cheap versions.

The woman stood up, walking towards the bar. 'Tell me something,' she said. 'If you knew where he was, and you'd identified him, why didn't you just end him? Why didn't you bring me his metaphorical carcass? It would've been better to show your allegiance to this. What have I got? Nothing. What reason could you have had for coming to me first?'

'Well, with everything that you went through out in Russia before your escape, maybe you would want to look him in the eye and finish him yourself. That would be a gift,' said Kirsten. 'But we are practical people. Holding Godfrey, trying to bring him to you while infiltrating your own ranks would not be easy, so clearly, that was out of the question. The other problem was Anna Hunt. She'd helped me find him and she'd put a watching brief on him. She would look after him for the first week. I would look after him for the second, and in the meantime, we would look and hunt for you. Keep Godfrey safe and kill you. Anna Hunt's out there watching him, makes it more difficult to kill him.'

'Anna Hunt's quite the operator,' she said, 'but I'll tell you who isn't an operator; Mark Lamb, he's a good bomber, but he's not very smart. Are you, Mr Lamb? Stand up.'

Mark Lamb stood up. He dwarfed the woman walking towards him. Kirsten realised that the woman wasn't wearing a dress, rather, it was a rather involved gown. And now, as she walked towards Mark Lamb, it opened at the front. Clearly, she'd been swimming, but the description of her had been accurate, for she had red flowing locks. Quite stunning.

'Tell me, Mr Lamb, what do you think of the story from our lady friend?'

'I wouldn't trust her,' said Mark Lamb. 'Held the gun to my head all the way here. Took out my people.'

'What about you, Craig? Do you believe in your former lover?'

'No,' he said. 'I don't. She was never like this. She would've taken it on herself, ended it herself.'

Gethsemane turned and looked at Kirsten, raising an eyebrow.

'The job changes people,' said Kirsten. 'When Craig left . . . when I was away and he then left, I realised who to blame for it all. Godfrey's betrayal led to Craig getting his legs blown off. That was what drove Craig down this well, and I thought to the blackest night, but not anymore. I've seen what it is, I've seen what's happened to the Service, I've seen how you've undercut it and tried to bring it back up. You might call me a believer,' she said. 'And Craig, look at him. I thought he was a

193

wreck; he's not. He's him again. Those things are helping; the mobility helps.'

'And so, what has brought you here?' asked Gethsemane. 'Simplify it for me. Bring it down to its core element.'

'I hate Godfrey for what he did to Craig. Hate him so much that I will see him dead. I can't see him dead because Anna Hunt's in the way. She's too good. I won't get past her. I'm very good, but she trained me. She ran me as her operative for many years. Anna is someone I need help to get past. If Godfrey and her are together, if he's alerted while I'm in the middle of doing the task, it won't work. I need Craig, and I need your help. I'm here to kill Godfrey.'

Craig nodded, walked up to Kirsten, and wrapped her up in his arms again. He kissed her deeply, repeatedly.

'Good,' said Gethsemane. 'I, however, have a problem. I'm not happy with how you got here. Not you; you have been ingenious. You have played people as a good operative should. Someone, however, should have stronger defences. I make my allies and I expect my allies to protect me, not to lead, potentially, some of my strongest enemies to me. Mr Lamb didn't know you had a change of heart. You could have been walking in here to kill me. Isn't that right, Mr Lamb?'

'I want you to kill him,' Gethsemane said, turning to Kirsten. 'I want you to put a bullet in his head. You can let him go into the pool. Don't make a mess on the side here.'

Mark Lamb went to run, but two men from the side, heavies who were standing by, grabbed him, forced him down to his knees, leaning over the swimming pool.

'I take it, you have a gun on you,' said Gethsemane. 'I've got one trained on you all the time. That's why we didn't take it off you, but please, use it now.'

Inside, Kirsten was in turmoil. She couldn't do this, but there was so much at stake. She couldn't kill Mark Lamb. Could she let him be killed? He wasn't innocent.

'I said I wanted Godfrey gone and I'll come for Godfrey and I'll help you kill him,' said Kirsten, 'but I told this man that if he brought me here, I would let him live. I'm a person of my word. So, I won't kill him.'

Gethsemane looked over at Craig, who gave a nod.

'Craig said you had a moral compass in you. He said it would take time for you to come round. He said you would struggle with what we were doing and how, and why. You'd have to see it for yourself. I admire that resolve. You're in a room of people who could just take you down, and all you have to do to make sure they don't, is kill this man. And he's nobody, is he? He's a bomber; he deserves to die. He hands us all these tools with which to kill and cause mayhem. You deserve to die, Mr Lamb, but this woman won't kill you. Say thank you to her.'

Mark Lamb's face was white. There were tears in his eyes. 'Thank you,' he said, croaking to get the words out. 'Thank you.'

'I, however,' said Gethsemane, 'feel betrayed and have an organisation to protect. When people as weak as you lead people in, we need to close that weakness. Oh, don't worry, Mr Lamb. I blame you entirely.'

Gethsemane pulled a gun out from the folds of her dressing gown and, from point-blank range, shot the man. He tumbled backwards into the swimming pool, but the spatter from the shot sent blood down the front of Gethsemane and the two men who were standing beside her. She spun round to everyone else, half-laughing.

'When will people learn?' she said. 'I don't take kindly to failure.'

Chapter 24

Kirsten stood at the rear of the house Gethsemane and her people were occupying. In a few moments, they would be on the road, making their way south to Skye and to Snizort. Godfrey awaited them there, as did Anna. Kirsten couldn't say she was coming. Anna would know from Justin that Kirsten was trying for contact. She would also know when Kirsten didn't respond. But what to make of that would be another matter.

Gethsemane had insisted that they travel as soon as possible, worried about Godfrey being on the move. It made sense to Kirsten. After all, nobody from Gethsemane's side was watching Godfrey.

There was a discreet cough behind her, and she turned to see Craig walking towards her. His new appendages still took some getting used to. The freedom they gave him was blowing Kirsten away. She turned back, looking out at the garden beyond her and the magnificent trees that sheltered the property from all onlookers.

'You've impressed her,' said Craig.

'I'm not here to impress her,' said Kirsten. She felt that if she came over too gushing about Gethsemane, that Craig would see through it.

'That couldn't have been pleasant for you,' he said.

'I've seen people die before. I have been in this job for a while.'

'You have, but your instinct would have been to save him, to say no. After all, you were the one who said you'd given him your word that you wouldn't kill him. You would let him live.'

'And I did.'

'But somebody else was going against that,' said Craig.

'Is she stable?' asked Kirsten.

It was a reasonable question and one she felt she had to ask because Craig would expect it from her. Kirsten was never one to simply toe the line. If she thought something was up, she would say. Craig needed to see the same person.

'She is.' His hands were now on her hips, pulling her close. 'Have you missed me?' he said.

'I've missed you since that day in Zante because you've been gone.'

He pulled himself close to her, and she felt his hands running up the inside of her T-shirt across her belly. She remembered that feeling. Remembered the excitement of those first contacts before they got truly intimate. They wouldn't be getting truly intimate now. There was no time. This was what she missed.

'I wish they'd left us alone in Zante,' she said.

'So do I. We could be ignorant of all this,' said Craig. 'And you would still see me as what you wanted. My full figure.' Kirsten grabbed his hands, pulled them out from under her T-shirt, and turned round.

'You never got that wasn't a problem. It wasn't the fact that your legs weren't there that ever caused me issues. You went missing. You went away. Not your legs.'

'I'm sorry,' he said. 'You're right; it took an awful lot. It took me a while to learn to hate the right people. To understand who was to blame. Now I do. Godfrey's to blame.'

When Kirsten heard those words, she understood because she blamed Godfrey as well. Admittedly, it hadn't driven her this far, but she understood.

'And of course, the Service,' said Craig. 'The Service also did this to me. That's why it has to come down.'

'How do we pick out what in the Service remains good?'

'Because they'll join us.'

Kirsten turned and walked away from Craig, and then she turned back. 'Those people, the men who wanted to take me, the woman that let it happen, are not good people. They're an evil in the Service as much as anything else. And just because they go on your side, they're okay?'

'A temporary thing,' said Craig, 'temporary until we . . .' He stopped, looking at her, his eyes running down her body. 'I'm so sorry,' he said, 'I could never have forgiven myself if they'd got to . . .'

Kirsten wanted to break down and cry. All the memories were flooding back to her about the incident, about being so vulnerable, but she didn't. Instead, she stared at him.

'You weren't there, and you didn't save me. Anna Hunt did. And now I'm going over there and she's going to get in the way. She's a good person; she's not the problem with the Service.'

'She would be an unfortunate casualty of war,' said Craig. He marched up to Kirsten, grabbed her roughly, and kissed her again. 'When we're running it, it'll be different. We're outside in two minutes,' he said. 'I was told to come and get you. Let's go.'

Kirsten watched him go and had to force herself not to cry. *Anna Hunt, an unfortunate casualty of war.* This wasn't Craig. This wasn't him. Was it?

And yet he still wanted her. He wanted her so badly she could feel it. And she could feel her response. Sometimes two things just slammed together, magnetised. They didn't repel; they were attracted, no matter what was going on around them.

It can't be, though, she thought. *It can't be.*

Kirsten stepped out of the room and walked to the front of the building. One car was there with Gethsemane in the rear, her red hair layered over her shoulders. Kirsten could see her because the door was open, although the windows were dark.

'You'll be joining me,' said Gethsemane. 'I think we need to talk.'

Kirsten was feeling a little worried, but she nodded and abruptly walked towards the car. She stopped for a moment looking for Craig and saw him get in the car further back. He smiled at her. Then she stepped inside.

It was a long run down to Skye, and it started in daylight. Gethsemane quizzed Kirsten the whole way down, getting her to replay in detail what had happened at Snizort. How things were looking on the land. How she realised Gethsemane was right. By the time they'd crossed the Skye Bridge, Kirsten had been peppered with questions. She believed she was still alive because her answers had been taken onboard as genuine. They pulled up close to Snizort. Gethsemane said nothing.

'It's that house over there towards the rear,' said Kirsten.

'And where's Anna Hunt?'

'Here somewhere,' said Kirsten. 'She'll be sitting, waiting, keeping a lookout.'

'What do you suggest we do?' she said.

'Personally,' said Kirsten, 'I wouldn't get close. Anna might have a rifle. Anna might use the darkness to her benefit. She's very good. I'd get a rocket launcher. Do you have one?'

'Yes,' said Gethsemane. 'We have one in the rear, but I don't like that plan.'

'Why? We won't get touched. Anna Hunt is well off. You can always check afterwards to see if Godfrey's in there—all the little bits.'

'You really don't like him, do you?' said Gethsemane. 'And I can understand that.'

Kirsten waited to see what the woman would say next. She was clearly thinking things through. And then she turned to Kirsten.

'No rockets. We'll attack him. We'll get close and we'll infiltrate the house.'

'Why?' asked Kirsten. 'You'll put yourself at risk with Anna Hunt.'

'Because we need to highlight his deeds.'

More like to know he's dead, thought Kirsten to herself. She gave a nod of approval to Gethsemane, who reeled down her window. A figure appeared beside her.

'We'll approach,' she said. 'Make sure they fan out, and make sure we get a positive identification before anyone kills him. We don't want several bodies lying around. It all becomes terribly untidy.'

Gethsemane stepped out of the car, and so Kirsten got out as well. In the dark, they crept forward, Gethsemane now in a tight jacket and jeans. She was clearly going to be part of the assault.

They ran forward carefully. Despite crouching low, gunfire

erupted. Several shots, one after another, saw many of Gethsemane's team suddenly fly backwards.

'He knew we were coming,' said Gethsemane.

Then she turned towards Kirsten. Kirsten saw the gun being pulled on her, grabbed her own out, then realised that there were no bullets in it. Gethsemane fired as Kirsten rolled away. Then she ran for all she was worth in the dark, zig-zagging left and right, jumping over hillocks and staying low.

As she got to the other side of the hillock for cover, she noticed a car departing the building. Godfrey was on the move.

'Get after him,' shouted Gethsemane.

Kirsten looked around and tried to run to the road, but she realised someone was now driving along in a car. It was moving at speed and the shooting had stopped. She put her hand out, looking for the car to slow down. The driver's door opened.

'Get the hell in.' It was Anna Hunt. Kirsten jumped into the car. 'There must be about four or five cars behind. Look. They're all leaving again.'

'Good shooting. How many did you get?' asked Kirsten.

'Seven, eight. How many more have we got?'

'Four, five. They've got three cars between them. Godfrey's off in one.'

They headed north through Skye, then turned left towards Dunvegan. As Kirsten and Anna Hunt raced along, they saw the cars had pulled off the main road, and looped towards Dunvegan Castle. As they reached it, there were cars in the car park. The people from the cars were running on foot, in towards the castle.

'Do we go in together?' asked Kirsten.

'No,' said Anna. 'I'll fan wide. Come around and behind. Just take them out, as many as we can. We'll have to trust Godfrey will be okay on his own. If we find him, we find him. Worst case, nobody walks out of here. That way, the secrets are safe.'

Just great, thought Kirsten. Then she tore off, not down the main path but towards the side. She found a blocked-up exit for the castle, and climbed the bars that were holding back her access, arriving inside.

Everywhere was dark. The stone fixture was dull in the darkness and gave an air of foreboding. There was no comfort here, just stone-cold terror. Her life was now part of a game of reactions. But then, wasn't it always these days?

She spread herself up against a wall, flicked her head around the corner, saw a shape, a shadow. Kirsten fired. The figure dropped. She'd got the height of it right. It wasn't Anna Hunt.

She heard noises. People heading upwards on stone steps. She heard more gunfire. Then she saw Gethsemane.

She was inside the building, making her way up the stone steps. Kirsten followed her carefully from behind. Soon, Kirsten reached the top of a spiralling staircase and came out on top of a roof. She saw Godfrey on the far side, looking down, wondering if he could jump, but Gethsemane was there. Craig was standing beside her.

'End of the line, dear Godfrey. End of the line. The one you left me on. It's taken me a while to find you, but this will be good. Would you rather I pushed you down there or blew your brains out?'

Kirsten stepped quietly onto the rooftop.

'You're not here for me,' said Godfrey. 'You're here for what I hold. Here for what secrets I know. You've taken Craig in. A right seductress she is, and a damn fool you are. She's taken you in. They want the secrets. But of course, you don't know about the secrets. You don't know that I operate entirely off the internet, entirely off any electronic system. I have proper records. But where? Enough details to bring the Service down.'

'He's lying,' said Gethsemane. 'He is lying.'

Kirsten could hear shots behind her. A man cried out, then another. That was at least three of them dead. Maybe there was another one to go. She wasn't sure. Did Anna's description include Craig?

'Don't,' said Kirsten suddenly. Put her arm out in front of her, the gun raised at Gethsemane.

'He's lying about this vault nonsense,' said the redheaded woman. 'Godfrey wouldn't store secrets that way. We should just kill him.'

Gethsemane went suddenly silent, and then Kirsten saw her readying to fire. Craig had pulled his gun out, pointing it at Kirsten.

'Don't believe him! Godfrey's a liar. He's causing all these problems. He's the one to blame.'

Kirsten saw Gethsemane go to shoot and fired. She hit the woman in the head. But a pain ripped through Kirsten's shoulder. Craig had fired, causing her to spin round onto the floor. She looked over and saw Craig pointing the gun down at her.

'Kirsten, I believed you,' he said. 'I was ready. I was . . .'

There was a shot, then another one, then two more, and Kirsten watched as Craig flew backwards across the rooftop. Standing at the stairs was Anna Hunt. She strode forward, looked down at Craig, and checked for a pulse.

'Well done, ladies,' said Godfrey. 'At least I have some people I can rely on. Gethsemane, eh? That's who she was.'

Anna Hunt walked quickly over to Godfrey. 'You knew exactly who she was. You left her behind. She's been right, the Service has gone down. It's not what it should be, and I blame the one who's running it.'

'We'll counterattack the Russians, though. Bring them to heel. Bring them into line,' said Godfrey. 'I won't let them attack the Service like this again. There will be a vengeance. We'll take back our Service. Now come on, the pair of you. Let's go.'

Anna Hunt raised her gun and pointed it at Godfrey's head. 'You're not fit for the Service,' she said and fired twice.

The blow knocked him backwards. If he hadn't been killed by the bullet, he would have died from the fall, as he tumbled off the roof of the Dunvegan Castle. Godfrey lay on the ground in a bloody mess.

Kirsten watched Anna Hunt standing and looking down from the top of the castle, tears welling in her eyes. Anna then turned, walked over to Kirsten, and helped her up. Her shoulder was bleeding.

'Let me look at that,' she said, but Kirsten shrugged her off, walked over, and put her hand down on Craig. There was no life in him. He was dead.

'He was going to shoot you. He'd have finished you. I told you to watch out for it.'

'I know he was going to shoot me. It doesn't make it any better.'

It took a while before there were sirens and police cars. Gunshots had been heard in the night, and Anna Hunt fielded the police as they arrived. Both Kirsten and she had put their guns down, but Kirsten hadn't left Craig. When he was taken away by the ambulance later that night, Kirsten let her tears flow properly. Craig was dead. She was trying to let him go, but she didn't want to.

Chapter 25

'Are you sure you're going to go?'

Anna Hunt posed the question while turning over the prawns on the barbecue. Kirsten was sitting in the intimate little garden of Anna Hunt's abode by Loch Ness. Justin was currently pouring a beer for himself and plunging a cafetière of coffee for Kirsten. Anna had a large goblet of red wine beside her.

'Mind's made up,' said Kirsten. 'I need time away. I need to work out what I'm going to do.'

I could really use your help,' said Anna. 'I'm intending to get the Service back up to strength. Finding a new leader will be a priority. I need to get the links established again that were torn apart. Also, I need to vet those who turned because some of them were good people taken in.'

'Is that wise?' asked Kirsten.

'You just don't dig agents up out of nowhere; takes time to train them. Time to bring them on. That's why I could do with you hanging about; even in a non-operational role. You could teach them spy craft. Teach them how to fight. Teach them the tools of the trade out there.'

'Sorry,' said Kirsten. 'I think I've done enough for my country for a while, and besides, I'm not sure I want to get back into that line.'

'Then what will you do?' asked Justin. 'You're not going freelance again, are you?'

'No. At least, certainly not at first. Need to spend some time with myself. I want to go somewhere that's warm, somewhere where I get time to think about things. I need to put Craig to rest. It's difficult when you've cared that much for someone, to watch them put a gun in your face, to know they were going to kill you.'

'I'm sure it wasn't,' said Justin. 'I wish I could have been there with you both.'

'You don't really,' said Anna. 'But I really get it, Kirsten. I'm building this Service back up and then I am leaving also.'

Justin's mouth literally fell open. 'But you are the Service at the moment,' he said.

'I'm never the Service. I might be the one to bring the Service to task but I'm not it. Need to find who is, though.'

'Did you want me to stay on to be that person?' asked Kirsten. 'Not that I'm offering.'

'You're too scrupulous. If you had to go a little on the dark side just to make things work, you couldn't live with yourself, so no. I never intended you to be head of the Service. You're an operative. You're a good one, maybe the best, but you're not material for the head of the Service.'

'That's a compliment I'm happy to take,' said Kirsten. She lifted a plate up, held it towards Anna, who dropped some prawns on the plate. Kirsten sat back down with it and greedily ate.

'You haven't asked,' said Anna. 'All the time afterwards, all the silence, you haven't asked.'

'You told everybody he got shot in the crossfire,' said Kirsten. 'You told everyone he was taken out. Why?'

'What are we talking about?' asked Justin.

'Godfrey,' said Kirsten. She looked at Anna, who gave a simple nod to let her know Justin could hear it. 'Godfrey didn't die at the hands of Gethsemane or Craig. We had saved him and then Anna shot him.'

Justin sat back in his chair for a moment and sipped his beer. 'Why?'

'Because they were right. All those operatives turned. That wasn't a lie. They could see it. They turned on Godfrey because he was over the line. He was operating in the wrong. He had to be taken out of the picture. Kirsten wouldn't have done that, so it fell to me.'

'But you and Godfrey were . . .'

'That's right, Mr Chivers; we were, but we were no longer. Not for a long time. It's been over the last lot of years that I've seen the change. I've had to stand by him because we couldn't disrupt the Service like that. But this was a chance; this was a chance after the turmoil. If we'd put him back in, none of those agents that turned would've come back and he would've hunted them. He would've closed every loop and put them in the ground.'

'What are you going to do? Call an amnesty?'

'What we're going to do,' said Anna, smiling at Chivers. 'We're going to meet each of them and we're going to find out why, and I'm going to see if they're worthy enough to come back in, see if they can be trusted. I've been in this game long enough to know people. Seen the bad turn good and the good turn bad. I told you, I'm going to get this Service back up on its feet. That's my job now, and when it is done, I will

209

walk.'

Kirsten picked up her coffee cup, poured in the coffee that Justin had pressed down, and then held her cup up.

'To Anna Hunt in her rebuilding plans,' she said. Anna smiled and tapped her glass and Kirsten's mug.

Justin raised his beer. 'May they be bloody quick for her,' said Kirsten.

'I hope so,' said Anna, 'but I doubt it. Where are you going anyway? You sticking around the UK?'

'No,' said Kirsten, 'I'm going somewhere. I don't know where. She reached into her back pocket, and took out an envelope. 'There are contact details so you can get me, you or Justin. If either of you ever needs me, I'm here. I wouldn't be here today without the pair of you, and if you have a time of need, I'll come.'

'Are you sure?' asked Anna. 'If you want to be totally out, I'm good with that.'

Kirsten put her drink down, stepped forward, hugged Anna, and then kissed her on the cheek.

'I never had a sister. Guess you're the closest I've ever had. I had a brother,' she said, turning to Justin, 'and he wasn't like you.' There was some light laughter. 'But us three, what we've been through, we're family. I won't see family lacking.'

They spent the rest of the afternoon around the barbecue until Kirsten said she had to go. Anna Hunt walked her to her car.

'I guess this is goodbye for a while,' said Anna. 'Pity but I don't begrudge you any of it.'

'You can get a hold of me. But, more importantly, deal with what happened to you out there,' said Kirsten. 'I wouldn't even know how to begin. Get yourself some professional help with that.'

'That's why I'm getting out,' said Anna. 'That's why I'm going to follow you. I sacrificed a lot for this country. In fact, I think I sacrificed too much. I was getting to a point where I wanted to head off to the sunset. I wanted someone close. Five, six years ago, I thought I might have had a chance at Godfrey once he retired from the job. But I saw him change, and now, I don't know. I don't know if I could ever be like that with someone after what's happened.'

'Get help,' said Kirsten. 'I'll reserve a beach towel for you. You can come and lie beside me when you're done. We can hit the town together. I think we cut quite a good look on the town, soon reel the men in.'

'I think those days are gone,' said Anna, laughing, 'but if you see anyone out there that's decent, drop me a line.'

Kirsten gave a hollow laugh. 'I guess this job took both our men away.'

'I guess so,' said Anna. 'Safe travels.

"Look after yourself, and anytime you want anything, I'm here, sister,' said Kirsten, and hugged Anna for the last time.

As she drove away, tears were streaming from her eyes, but she had another appointment to make, one that she wasn't looking forward to. Anna was of an age that she may see her again, but she also was a colleague. Yes, now a close friend, but she hadn't been the one to be her true mentor. She would see him for one last time.

She parked up in Inverness and wandered along to the coffee shop that she knew he liked. It was a fair enough call because the coffee was good, and she sat down at a table awaiting his arrival. She had contacted the police station, asked the team to send him out for coffee, which wasn't easy when he was a DCI.

But she told Hope it was important and Hope did as asked. Macleod arrived at the counter and announced an order of coffee that was wholly ridiculous. He was told by the assistant that what he was looking for was on the table behind him. He turned around, his shoulders sagging, and then he saw her.

Kirsten saw the uplift in his shoulders. He strode over to the table, and she stood up. They embraced, and then he sat down.

'What do you want?' he asked.

'Coffee's coming. I needed to see you because . . . ' she stopped and he looked at her.

'You're going away,' he said. 'What happened?'

'I can't talk to you about stuff like that.'

'There was a kerfuffle at Dunvegan Castle on Skye. Something big happened. Was Craig involved?'

Kirsten nodded.

'He's dead.'

She nodded again.

'I'm so sorry,' said Macleod, 'I know you loved him.' And then the older man stopped and stared into her face. 'And he betrayed you.' She shook her head. 'No,' he said, 'he tried to kill you. You didn't have to?'

Again, she shook her head. 'I need you to watch the flat,' said Kirsten suddenly. 'I might be back one day, but I'm going away.'

'Undercover work?'

Kirsten shook her head. 'I'm going away for me. I'm going to find out what I want to do.'

'Do you regret it?' asked Macleod.

Kirsten shook her head. 'You were right, and a lot of it I loved. Just need time away. I need time to process. I need time

212

to go and . . .'

'Grieve,' said Macleod. 'You need to grieve.' The coffees arrived and the pair of them sat there looking at each other.

'How's police work going?' she asked him. 'DCI, I see now. You haven't let them kick you upstairs? Never let them take you off that meaningful bit. You just get lots of paperwork. . . . I heard you had some issues.'

'Issues?' he said and laughed. 'There's somebody over at the table, two over from us.' Kirsten looked. There was no one there. 'He wears a monk's habit, and he follows me around. He's not real, but he's real up here.'

'I'm sorry,' she said.

'I'm not. It's like yourself. I've loved the job. Maybe I need time out. Maybe I need to catch a breath. I always thought Hope would be ready, and there she is, detective inspector. I would leave and the DCI above her would work with her. Our DCI's messed up. There was a vacancy; they persuaded me.'

'I'll be about one day,' said Kirsten. 'Be here.'

'I've got Jane. I'm not going anywhere. If you need any advice or if you just want to talk it through with some old man, I'm always here for you.'

Tears fell from Kirsten's face. She stood up and hugged him, and then turned and downed her coffee. She saw him laugh.

'With the way you are about coffee, I'm not leaving a good one there. You would complain to me.' She cried again. 'I'll see you!'

She walked out of the coffeehouse, not once looking back because she knew she wouldn't leave. It was time to go away. It was time to head off, time to find herself. She just hoped Macleod would still be alive when she got back. She didn't know how long it was going to take her, and she didn't know

213

where it was going to take her, but she'd find what she wanted. Kirsten had to. Everything else was gone.

Epilogue

T he woman sat on the beach, her long legs out in front of her, the sun baking down. Sweat was rolling off her body, mixed in with suntan lotion, and she watched as the men surreptitiously took glances towards her. They would stand and parade, and she enjoyed seeing their hunger, their desire for her. Beside her was a tequila and an enormous sun hat, which she'd taken off to allow her hair to spray over her shoulders.

This was the life. This is where she wanted to be adored, loved. And then she saw a woman walking along the sand. The woman seemed to have a sense of purpose. It intrigued the sunbather so much so that she grabbed a T-shirt and pulled it on, standing up from her sun lounger to see where the woman went.

The day was boiling, and yet the purposeful woman wore a shirt with what looked like a gym crop top underneath. She was wearing three-quarter-length pants, bare feet in the sand, with a bag thrown over her shoulder. Her hair was tied up at the back, but what struck the woman was the swagger.

It was a happy swagger. It was a woman who was where she wanted to be. Some men looked at her, but she didn't notice them. She just kept walking.

The sunbather put on her flip-flops, raced across the sand, and watched the purposeful woman go up to the steps at the end of the beach. The woman strode right and then left and marched along the street by the shore. Next, the purposeful woman turned down a set of steps that had many men hanging around them. The men looked a rough sort, not the sort that you would want to get involved with, but the sunbather's fascination spurred her on.

The sunbather walked past the men as they threw comments about her figure and about what she could do for them. The sunbather ignored them, watching the woman ahead disappear down into a dimly lit room. There was a cacophony of noise inside. Unexpectedly, the purposeful woman stopped.

She dug into her bag and produced a mask, tying it around her face. The purposeful woman then looked back, making sure no one could see her, but caught the sunbather who was following her. A wide smile broke out and the sunbather in her flip-flops needed to follow her.

The now masked woman pushed open a set of double doors and the noise rose to a new level. There were cheers. There were whoops and cries. The sunbather entered the room but no eyes were on her. They were all on the masked woman.

The masked woman took off her shirt and then dropped her three-quarter-length pants. Underneath, she had tight shorts on and she reached into her bag, pulling out gloves that covered her knuckles. Before her was a ring of sorts, eight sides. The sunbather could barely see above the crowd, so she worked her way up some tiered seating and got to the top.

This was unusual. She was in a room of men, for they all looked like men, except for the masked woman donning the gloves. Inside the ring was a man that must have been close to seven feet tall. He was built out of sheer muscle.

She watched as someone handed him a large watermelon, which he threw into the air and then slapped both palms against it as it came down. The thunderous clap exploded the watermelon across the floor of the ring. He started shouting something in the local language. The sunbather thought the translation was 'Your head'.

On the other side of the ring, the masked woman had stepped inside. She looked quite calm, simply grinning at the taunts that were coming from the other side of the ring. There was a referee who came up to them to tell them how to fight, but the large man swatted him away. Blood poured from the referee's mouth and he took off out of the ring. The sunbather doubted there would be any rules, and she feared for the masked woman's safety.

A minute later, it was all over and the sunbather was trying to work out what had happened. The masked woman had moved so quick. She had hit the man so many times from all angles, and when he had fallen, going down like the largest tree trunk ever seen, the ring had vibrated. The masked woman was still standing. She had taken a couple of punches from the giant, faced some hits that you would've thought would've broken her jaw.

She had blood dripping from her mouth, but she didn't seem to care. Instead, a small man entered the ring and handed her what looked like a significant amount of money. She stepped out of the ring surrounded by the men and put the money in her bag. Dressing herself again, the masked woman headed towards the back of the room and into a locker area. It looked small, but had the word 'female' above it. The sunbather followed her, the only person who did so, for everyone else was a man.

She watched as the masked woman opened the locker and pushed the door back. She picked up a photograph, staring at it carefully before putting it back on the inside of the locker. There was a second photograph as well. The masked woman reached inside the locker, took out a brush, let her hair out, and brushed it. She took the mask off to do so and turned to watch the sunbather.

The sunbather stepped forward and asked if she could see the photographs. The female fighter didn't seem to understand fully, so the sunbather pointed. The sunbather looked and saw a group of people. The female fighter looked younger in the photograph, and she was wearing a policewoman's uniform from a different country. Beside her was another young man, a woman who was tall with red hair, and an old man. The fighter said something about it then showed with her arms that they were some sort of unit.

There was another photograph. This was a man, but he had the face of a boy. A face that showed the understanding of a three-year-old. The female fighter said the word 'brother' in the local language. The sunbather saw the tear in the woman's eye. Maybe the brother wasn't around anymore.

The fighter closed the locker door, gave a smile, and then left the female changing. For a moment, the sunbather was going to follow, but she guessed she had got most of the story. The only thing she didn't have was the woman's name.

She turned and looked at the locker, and there was a name written on it. The first part of the name was unfamiliar. So was the second part. Not names from these parts, so she walked to the door of the changing and asked one man who the masked woman was.

He said 'The Shadow' but in their own language. He said she calls herself 'The Shadow', but she has another name, her own name. The woman asked what it was, and the man said he couldn't remember because it was awkward to say. So, the woman turned back into the female changing room, and put her finger up, and ran it across the name that was written there.

Seorasina Macleod.

The sunbather stepped back and thought about the photograph she'd seen. *Just who was this woman? So confident in herself, yet so strong. Able to handle herself, and happy to be in such fights. The Shadow!*

She would come back to see 'The Shadow' again.

Read on to discover the Patrick Smythe series!

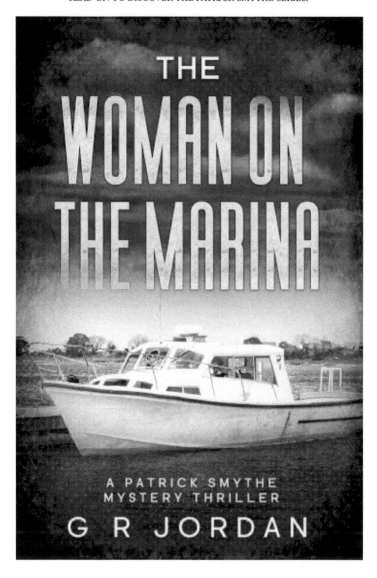

THE
WOMAN ON
THE MARINA

A PATRICK SMYTHE
MYSTERY THRILLER

G R JORDAN

Patrick Smythe is a former Northern Irish policeman who

after suffering an amputation after a bomb blast, takes to the sea between the west coast of Scotland and his homeland to ply his trade as a private investigator. Join Paddy as he tries to work to his own ethics while knowing how to bend the rules he once enforced. Working from his beloved motorboat 'Craigantlet', Paddy decides to rescue a drug mule in this short story from the pen of G R Jordan.

Join G R Jordan's monthly newsletter about forthcoming releases and special writings for his tribe of avid readers and then receive your free Patrick Smythe short story.

Go to https://bit.ly/PatrickSmythe for your Patrick Smythe journey to start!

About the Author

GR Jordan is a self-published author who finally decided at forty that in order to have an enjoyable lifestyle, his creative beast within would have to be unleashed. His books mirror that conflict in life where acts of decency contend with self-promotion, goodness stares in horror at evil, and kindness blindsides us when we at our worst. Corrupting our world with his parade of wondrous and horrific characters, he highlights everyday tensions with fresh eyes whilst taking his methodical, intelligent mainstays on a roller-coaster ride of dilemmas, all the while suffering the banter of their provocative sidekicks.

A graduate of Loughborough University where he masqueraded as a chemical engineer but ultimately played American football, Gary had worked at changing the shape of cereal flakes and pulled a pallet truck for a living. Watching vegetables freeze at -40'C was another career highlight and he was also one of the Scottish Highlands "blind" air traffic controllers.

These days he has graduated to answering a telephone to people in trouble before telephoning other people to sort it out.

Having flirted with most places in the UK, he is now based in the Isle of Lewis in Scotland where his free time is spent between raising a young family with his wife, writing, figuring out how to work a loom and caring for a small flock of chickens. Luckily, his writing is influenced by his varied work and life experience as the chickens have not been the poetical inspiration he had hoped for!

You can connect with me on:

🌐 https://grjordan.com

🅵 https://facebook.com/carpetlessleprechaun

Subscribe to my newsletter:

✉ https://bit.ly/PatrickSmythe

Also by G R Jordan

G R Jordan writes across multiple genres including crime, dark and action adventure fantasy, feel good fantasy, mystery thriller and horror fantasy. Below is a selection of his work. Whilst all books are available across online stores, signed copies are available at his personal shop.

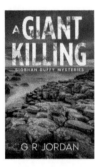

A Giant Killing: Siobhan Duffy Mysteries #1
https://grjordan.com/product/a-giant-killing
A body lies on the Giant's boot. Discord, as the master of secrets has been found. Can former spy Siobhan Duffy find the killer before they execute her former colleagues?

When retired operative Siobhan Duffy sees the killing of her former master in the paper, her unease sends her down a path of discovery and fear. Aided by her young housekeeper and scruff of a gardener, Siobhan begins a quest to discover the reason for her spy boss' death and unravels a can of worms today's masters would rather keep closed. But in a world of secrets, the difference between revenge and simple, if brutal, housekeeping becomes the hardest truth to know.

The past is a child who never leaves home!

Jac's Revenge (A Jack Moonshine Thriller #1)
https://grjordan.com/product/jacs-revenge

An unexpected hit makes Debbie a widow. The attention of her man's killer spawns a brutal yet classy alter ego. But how far can you play the game before it takes over your life?

All her life, Debbie Parlor lived in her man's shadow, knowing his work was never truly honest. She turned her head from news stories and rumours. But when he was disposed of for his smile to placate a rival crime lord, Jac Moonshine was born. And when Debbie is paid compensation for her loss like her car was written off, Jac decides that enough is enough.

Get on board with this tongue-in-cheek revenge thriller that will make you question how far you would go to avenge a loved one, and how much you would enjoy it!

Highlands and Islands Detective Thriller Series

https://grjordan.com/product/waters-edge

Join stalwart DI Macleod and his burgeoning new DC McGrath as they look into the darker side of the stunningly scenic and wilder parts of the north of Scotland. From the Black Isle to Lewis, from Mull to Harris and across to the small Isles, the Uists and Barra, this mismatched pairing follow murders, thieves and vengeful victims in an effort to restore tranquillity to the remoter parts of the land.

Be part of this tale of a surprise partnership amidst the foulest deeds and darkest souls who stalk this peaceful and most beautiful of lands, and you'll never see the Highlands the same way again.

Milton Keynes UK
Ingram Content Group UK Ltd.
UKHW011000080124
435661UK00001B/26

9 781915 562548